# The Realm of Eddie Ross

Ashley Burgoyne

ISBN: 9798450683256

Front and back cover by Jadzia Burgoyne

Map illustration by Wesley Burgoyne

The author would like to thank Melissa Collin for all her time, effort and assistance in bringing this book into existence.

ashleyburgoyne.wixsite.com/writerandcomposer

"Everything may not be quite as it seems…"

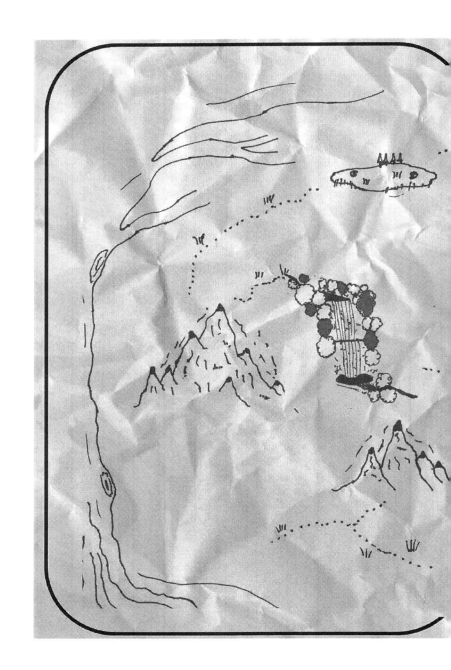

# Chapter One

'Go on; you can do it!'

Can I? Can I really do it this time?

'Nearly there Eddie, nearly there.'

The voice rings around my head. I *am* nearly there.

'Ohhhh.'

Not again.

'Bad luck, Eddie.'

'Yeah, bad luck mate.' Chris pats me on the back as he walks away.

'Isn't anyone gonna measure it?' I say.

'If it's below my line then it ain't a winner, is it?' *He's* here. I wondered how long it would take for him to appear.

'Hello Brian, how long you been here?'

'I've been watching you from the back.'

'It was close, wasn't it?'

'It was *way* off.'

'Not really.' Am I trying to irritate him, or what? 'Just a few inches off.'

'Here you go again with the inches. What is it with you and bleeding inches? One metre 45 centimetres. That's your target and don't you forget it.' He gives me a shove on the shoulder as he walks past muttering 'him and his bleeding inches.'

'Bad luck!' It's Carrot, my best friend.

'You're getting closer; definitely!'

Everyone else is wandering down the hill.

'Have you got the tape measure?' I frantically say to Carrot. 'We gotta measure it before the mark disappears.'

'It's here somewhere.' Carrot starts to pat every pocket on his commando-style jacket. He reminds me of my dad's best man in the video of their wedding. We timed him taking 3 minutes 10 seconds to find the wedding rings in his pocket. He claims to this day that it was something to do with the lining, whereas my mum always tells him it was something to do with the stag do the night before! With Carrot it's neither of these. Just pockets.

'Come on, it's going!' The anxiety in my voice works.

'Got it. I thought it was in the inner right arm upper pocket, but it was round in the back hidden mid-waist pocket.'

I stare at him. 'Are you sure you didn't get a manual with that jacket?'

'I just know these things.'

There's a pause as I wonder why he has put so much effort in to learning such facts. Carrot's probably now thinking that his nights of studying have paid off, having suitably impressed me.

'You'll thank me one day for all of these pockets!'

I don't reply. I just grab the tape measure and go to the wall.

'Quick, get the end and hold it on the ground.'

I pull out the tape measure that proudly says five metres on its chrome casing. I wish.

'How far from Brian's 1 metre 45 are you?'

'I've told you before, Carrot, it's 4 feet 9 inches.'

'Sorry.'

We've had this conversation so many times. For this exercise we must work in feet and inches. It's five maths lessons a week with Mr Evans that makes it difficult for Carrot to even say the word 'feet.' "Metres and centimetres boy," he would snort. "This is the 21st century where this once great nation is alone once more, having once been a slice of a bigger pie known as Europe." Three times he's done that speech and each time we seem to end the lesson doing pie charts!

'Four foot four,' I mutter.

'Never mind.'

'Just eight more inches.'

'Eight? I know I'm not the best at maths, but surely anything over five will do?'

He's right, of course, but there's more to this than just peeing up a wall. I think that I'm going to tell Carrot. But, unless I have any proof, I think that even Carrot, who I've known since I was five, will laugh at me.

'Of course,' I say with a pretend sort of confused expression on my face. 'It's all this metres, centimetres, feet and inches stuff. I just got in a muddle.'

Carrot smiles a smile as if to say "I'm not the only one who gets confused then."

'Five inches to go.'

*

To Carrot this isn't any more than just peeing up a wall. It is just that. Peeing up a wall.

For three years now Big Brian has held the record. He set his 1 metre 45 (4 foot 9) about six months ago, beating his own record by one centimetre (approximately 3/8 of an inch.) I've been challenging him for almost a year now and I've improved from a laughable three feet (and trust me, they did laugh) up to my new high of 4 foot 4. I am the number one contender, but until I beat his record Brian is going to keep his flies done up.

"Why should I keep beating my own record? It's getting a bit tedious" he's been heard to say. Tedious? Brian's been reading the dictionary again!

'Of course, it's all relative' says Carrot as we wander down the hill.

I look at him.

'You know, relative to size,' he continues.

I look down at my flies.

'No, not that,' he chuckles, 'well, maybe that, but your overall size,' he pauses, 'and age.'

He's right, once more. Carrot may appear a bit dafter than the next boy, not wholly due to his ginger hair (or indeed his over-pocketed action-man jacket), but he is invariably correct when it comes down to observation.

'I mean, how old is he now?'

'Fourteen.'

'Fourteen?'

'Yeah.'

Carrot shakes his head.

'You're not gonna still be doing this when you're 14, are you Eddie?'

'No way.' I say this a bit more vehemently than I intend to. After all, do you really think I want to be peeing up a wall just to beat Big Brian? There is so much more to this. 'I'm sticking to the rules.'

The rules are as follows:

    1)   You must be a boy (?)

    2)   You must be in year 7.

Brian is ok on rule one (I know, trust me), but he's in year 9. And he's one of the oldest in his year. It's just that there is only one thing in his life that he's ever come first in and this is it. Sad really. Having to expose himself in the woods just to be the best at something. Me? Well, I'm in the top set for everything at school. I'm not the best in any of the subjects, but I'm close in some... science; maths. Brian is the bottom of the bottom. In fact, he's dropped out of the bottom of some classes. They don't scrape the bottom of the barrel for him, they lift it up and he's usually found somewhere underneath.

'How tall is he?' inquires Carrot.

'About six foot.'

'Six foot?'

'Yeah.' I pull the tape measure out of its casing once more. 'Or 1 metre 83!'

Carrot laughs at my mathematical jesting.

'And how tall are you?'

'Five foot.' Too quick. I answered that question too quickly. How many 11 year-olds know their height straight away, and in feet and inches?

'How d'you know that?' Carrot enquires.

See, I told you I answered that too quickly. Now I'm going to have to lie to my best friend.

'It was in maths a couple of months ago,' I smile as I lie through my teeth. 'We had to measure our heights for one of Mr Evans' pie charts.'

'Did we? I don't remember.'

Idiot, he's in my maths class! Think boy, think.

'It was when you were on holiday. We spent all week on it.'

'Oh, back in March, when we were in our apartment in Porto?'

'Yes, that's it!'

'Oh, right.'

He seems satisfied with my explanation. Thank God for second homes!

'The chart wasn't in feet and inches, was it?'

'Eh?'

'You knew your height "in imperial and not metric".' This last bit comes out in a sort of Lancastrian accent, supposedly to sound like Mr Evans, I guess.

'You know me, Carrot, preferring "imperial to metric".' Mine comes out a bit more like a Geordie.

We laugh. I unravel the tape measure once more.

'Anyway, it's better knowing that you're exactly five feet tall rather than,' I turn the tape over hoping that the conversion doesn't present me with a nice round figure, '1 metre 52 point 4 centimetres!'

We laugh again. Phew! I hate telling lies to Carrot. But in eight inches' time I will be able to tell him the truth.

\*

'Becky saw you,' are the words I'm greeted with as I enter the living room.

'Becky saw you,' she repeats gleefully.

'I heard you the first time, Liz.'

Liz is my sister. She's 14. She's in Big Brian's year, but, like me, she's in all the top sets so she probably sees less of Brian than I do.

'Aren't you bothered that Becky saw what you were doing up in the woods?'

I look at Carrot, who's come around for tea.

'I didn't see any girls Eddie, honestly.'

Carrot is my personal look-out when I'm doing the wall thing. Everyone has their own look-out. Brian has skinny Trev. Pete "I can't get over 1 metre 20 (3 feet 11 and ¼)" Hughes has his brother Ian and Darren Trent relies on Darren Carter. The lads also huddle around in a tight semi-circle so no one can see the event taking place. I also hold my hands in such a fashion that I don't think anyone can see any of me, unlike Brian who proudly waves his round willy-nilly. He *is* six feet tall!

'What did Becky see?' I try not to sound worried, but I am, just a bit.

'Nothing!'

'Nothing?'

'Yes, exactly! Ha, ha.' She pokes me in the arm as she goes in to the kitchen.

'If she saw nothing, why did she say she saw something?' Carrot has missed the 'sizeist' wit of my sister.

'Just think yourself lucky that you don't have a sister,' is all I say to him.

He looks puzzled.

Puzzled is not an expression ginger-haired people should do. It doesn't *go*. Mind you, angry and ginger is even worse. The red of the cheeks really clashes with what's above. Not that Carrot gets angry often. He's grown used to his hair, which is good seeing as that colour is going to grow in parts he won't want it to. His real name is Derek Dickinson. But he's been Carrot for as long as I can remember him. Mind you, with a name like Derek Dickinson I think Carrot is an escape. Of course, teachers still call him Derek. He visibly cringes at the sound. The music and art teachers both call him Carrot, which he likes, whereas Mr "metric not imperial" Evans calls him Dickinson all the time. He calls us all by our surnames, which I don't mind because Ross can be a first or last name, so when he shouts my name out it never seems to have the impact he intends it to have. Thanks Dad.

'What's for tea?' asks Carrot.

'I don't know. What's for tea?' I call out to the kitchen.

'Mum's working late, she left a message on the machine. We've got to help ourselves.'

'What are you making then?' I rather wishfully, and somewhat cheekily, call out to Liz. She walks back in to the living room sipping from a can of Coke.

'The message says "help yourself", not, "Liz, make little Eddie his tea". I left the message on there. Listen to it yourself if you don't believe me.'

I decide against it, just in case she says something embarrassing on it that I don't want Carrot to hear.

'What are you having then?'

'Nothing,' says Liz. 'I'm going round Becky's for tea. See ya later.'

She grabs her jacket and leaves, calling behind her 'I think there's a pizza in the freezer. Bung that in if you can manage.' She slams the front door.

'Pizza?'

Oh no, here comes the Carrot pizza problem again.

'What sort is it?' he asks.

'I don't know. I didn't even know we had a pizza until just now.'

'It won't have anchovies on it, will it?'

Here comes the rash bit.

'Anchovies bring me out in a rash.'

Let me think, will it be the olives next or the pineapple? I'll plump for the olives.

'Will it have pineapple on it?'

Damn! So near, yet, so far.

'I still don't know, Carrot,' I say as we head for the freezer.

'And you know I hate olives.'

Hurrah! I knew you wouldn't let me down.

'I know you hate olives, Carrot.' Come to think of it, I don't think I know anyone who likes olives. I open the freezer. Carrot takes a step back as if he's not sure whether it's going to suck him in or not.

'You ok?' I ask him.

'Sure. It's just that I'm a bit wary of freezers after I had a dream about one the other night.'

'Really, what happened?' I try not to sound too excited, in case Carrot's dream was actually a nightmare and I don't want to sound over-excited by someone else's unfortunate night thoughts.

'I can't remember much. I just went in to a big freezer to get a cheese and tomato pizza out –' oh no, pizzas again '– and the door closed behind me.'

'What happened next?' I'm now starting to sound a little bit excited, but Carrot's got quite engrossed in his storytelling so I don't think he's noticed.

'Well,' he continues, 'these four orange-coloured lollies lit up in the four corners of the freezer, like Belisha beacons –' ah, now I'm getting a bit worried. I'm not sure I want him to carry on with this now '– then these toppings started to appear.'

'Toppings?'

'Yeah, pizza toppings.' Good grief. 'They came at me from all angles; pineapple slices, anchovies, olives and mushrooms.'

'Mushrooms? But you like mushrooms!'

'Exactly!'

'Then what happened?' I'm really sounding excited now 'coz I want to know which topping got to him first and what it did to him.

'Nothing.'

'Nothing?'

'Well, my mum came in and turned the light on. It felt like she had opened the freezer door and saved me; what with the light coming on.'

We stand and stare at the freezer. Something is going to happen to me quite soon and my chosen accomplice, although he doesn't know that he is, has a phobia of freezers.

'I'm going in!' I say trying to lighten the moment. Carrot holds his breath.

'It's ham and mushroom,' I say, 'no anchovies, no pineapple and no olives.'

'It's got mushrooms on it though,' shivers Carrot.

'But I thought we'd already discussed the fact that you like mushrooms.'

'I do, but, you know, after that dream....'

'Look, mate' I say as I put my hand on his shoulder, 'think of it as a way of getting the mushrooms back.'

'How do you mean?'

'Well, you're gonna eat them, aren't you? That's as good a way of any to destroy something; digesting it!'

Carrot laughs, nervously, and as I put the oven on I hope that my apparent bravado, compared to that of Carrot, will work on other things and not just on dreams of killer pizzas.

\*

'It's funny this, isn't it Eddie?' Carrot's holding my carved wooden box that I keep on my bedside table. I'm turning on my PS4 for a quick game whilst the pizza's cooking.

'What's funny about it?'

'The fact that it's a solid block of carved wood, yet it's so light, suggesting that it's in fact hollow.' I told you that Carrot, besides all his weird pizza hang-ups, is very observant. 'But what would be the point of it being hollow? You can't get into it.'

'Yes, I know, I've often thought that. Maybe it's some light South American wood?'

'Maybe.' He puts it down and picks up his PS4 controller.

Of course, I made up the South American wood bit, because, as with peeing up the wall, I haven't quite got it right yet. I know it's a box, or at least I think it is. I call it a box. Yet, it does appear to be just a light block of wood.

I win most of the ensuing races. Carrot always says that once he's got the same console and can practise as much as me, he'll win. He might. Carrot overcomes his temporary mushroom fear to triumph over the crispy, but not burnt, pizza. A bowl of ice cream follows, proudly retrieved from the freezer by the braver Carrot, and soon my mum comes home and Carrot leaves. I wash up and Mum's tired from the overtime so I leave her dozing on the sofa as I make my way to bed. Dad's not going to be home from his conference for a few more days yet.

I sit on my bed and hold my carved wooden box. I'm looking at the carvings as the box begins to feel warm. It's done this a couple of times before. It scared me then and it scares me now. I put it down and pull the duvet over me. I need to dream. Not Carrot-like pizza dreams, but serious, mind-jogging dreams. I can't remember something. I don't know what, but something is there, hiding from me in the corner of my mind. Pieces have appeared in dreams before, I'm sure, but I always forget them by sunrise. Nothing ever appears during the day. I need a dream that I can hold on to. Bring on the night!

# Chapter Two

It was there. I had it. It all came to me in the middle of the night. I sat bolt upright. Everything was clear. The room was warm. There was a glow from my wooden box. Maybe it was this giving off the heat? Then… nothing. It went. I mean, I think I just fell back to sleep. Why didn't I try and write it all down? All the thoughts that were filling my head. Making it feel like it would be more comfortable if it would just go ahead and explode. Maybe that was it. Overload! Too much information all at one time so my brain sent me back to sleep before it did explode. Well, you know, not actually explode so that my brains splattered all over my Pokémon wallpaper and Luton Town duvet cover (actually, I really think I've outgrown Pokémon, so a bit of brain goo might look ok on the walls. Do you think I could get the explosion to hit the walls but avoid the duvet?) but just send me back to sleep to avoid a brain haemorrhage, or at least a headache.

It's getting nearer though. I feel that the box thing is waiting for me to reach the 5-foot mark on the wall. It's bursting out, but it needs me to reach the right height on the wall before it can burst out.

That's it! *Bursting.* I need to be bursting to beat the record. I need to drink and drink and drink and not go to the toilet until I am facing that wall tonight.

\*

'What's relative mean?'

'Sorry, Brian?'

'What's relative mean?'

Brian has just walked all the way through the year 7s on the playground to ask me this. The rest of the year moved out of his way as he lumbered amongst them. He reminded me of something. A sort of cross between Moses parting the waves, Gulliver in Lilliput and an episode of Walking with Dinosaurs.

'Why do you ask me?'

Brian tends to only leave his base, the canteen, if he's going to beat someone up. So, I was treading carefully.

''Coz you were in the sentence I heard, that's why.'

I look at Carrot. He looks at me. We are clearly sharing the same light bulb that you get above your head when something clicks. Somebody else has been discussing our heights up the wall. Saying, like Carrot did, that it's all relative to size and age. I assume that they came to the same conclusion as us, saying that 4 foot 9 for a 6-foot-tall boy isn't as good as 4 foot 4 for a 5-foot-tall boy. It's all relative, isn't it?

'They're like your cousins, aren't they Eddie?' Carrot looks deadpan. We've only been chatting a few minutes so I'm not sure if it's daft pizza-fearing Carrot who's talking to me today or the much sharper "I don't remember measuring our height in maths" Carrot.

'That's right; cousins, relatives, aunts and uncles, all the same thing!'

Carrot smiles. It's the sharp Carrot.

'You must have some relatives, Brian?'

Now you're pushing it, Carrot.

'Yeah, I got a famous one.'

Carrot and I exchange glances. This is going to be good.

'He's a footballer.'

'Really? Who's he play for?'

People are starting to stare at the three of us now. I don't know whether people are impressed because we're standing right next to Brian and he hasn't hit us yet, or whether they think we're sad because we're holding a conversation with Big Brainless Brian in the middle of the year 7 playground.

'Scarborough.'

'Really?' says Carrot. He's got no idea about football. He was born, like me, in Luton, yet he's one of those Man. United "fans." Besides all the obvious questions with regards to having some sense of loyalty to where you were born, plus having visited the town/city, not to mention the ground and, dare I say it, actually see a match "live", the shirt clashes horribly with his hair. I tell him that the Luton kit was designed for him, the orange is perfect, but the ginger glory-seeker is happy to live 200 miles away from "his club", never see them play and clash with their over-priced, yearly changed strip as long as they win a trophy. "But that's just it," I tell him, "it's them winning the trophy, not you, 'coz you haven't been a part of the process." He tends just to sit, when I say this to him, and clash.

'So, non-league football then?' I say to Brian. Carrot looks suitably impressed. I knew he had no idea which league Scarborough was in.

'Yeah, but he played for them when they were in the league as well.'

Brian knows his stuff.

'Was he playing for them the year they got relegated to the Conference.'

'Yeah.'

I smile to myself. I bet he was a defender. They drop out of the football league with a member of Brian's family in the team. He must have been a defender. Dare I ask him, though?

'What position did he play in?' Ok. There's the bait. Please say defender, you'll make my day.

'Goalie.' Oh, fantastic. My expectations surpassed by Big Brian. *The goalie!*

'How tall is he?' No Carrot. Cherish the moment.

'Just under two metres.' Carrot looks at me.

'About 6 foot 6.' I say.

'Right,' says Carrot, looking suitably pleased with his contribution to the conversation.

There's a pause. Not an uncomfortable pause, just a pause.

'See ya later, then,' says Brian, 'and thanks for telling me what relative means. I think I learned more from you than I ever have in one of my lessons.'

That's because you've just talked to us for longer than you tend to stay in any of your lessons!

'Blimey, praise from Brian!' chirps Carrot. 'He might even concede that your height is relatively higher than his!'

'Don't hold your breath!'

*

'You don't look too good,' is what Carrot says to me on the way home.

'Don't I?'

'No, you're walking a bit strange.'

'Am I?'

'Nothing to do with PE last thing is it?'

It's got everything to do with PE. Practising the long jump *and* the high jump when you're desperate for the toilet. Not recommended.

'It's ok, Carrot. I just need the loo.'

'Wanna go to the wall and give it a shot?' he laughs.

'I intend to, but not now. Later.'

'You'll make yourself ill if you don't go when you need to.'

It's sometimes hard to forget that Carrot's dad's a doctor.

'I'll be ok. Can we meet up at the wall after tea, about 8 o'clock?'

'Sure, but it won't count.'

'Sorry?'

'If you beat Brian's record it won't count. You gotta have two independent witnesses.'

It's sometimes hard to forget that Carrot's mum's a lawyer. But it is true, it is another rule. I didn't mention it earlier because anyone who wants to have a go at the wall always attracts a crowd so witnesses aren't a problem. It's time to own up. Well; a bit, anyway.

'Can you forget about the record and just meet me at the wall at 8?' I make a sort of sheepish grin.

'Ok, if you want. Are you gonna pee before we meet up or are you still gonna do it up the wall?'

'Still up the wall, why?'

14

'That's four hours mate. You won't make it up the hill limping like that!' he chuckles.

'I will. Just be there.'

*

I sit cross-legged for most of the evening. Liz points it out to my mum who says it's very mature. Liz just laughs. After dinner I dash upstairs (well, it's more of a crawl really) to get myself sorted. I dress appropriately, coat etc., and pick up my wooden box. It warms up in my hands again. Is that a good sign, or bad? I shove it inside my coat. I tell Mum that I'm nipping round to Carrot's. "I want you back no later than 9.30" she says as I leave the house.

Carrot's right. The hill is very difficult to climb when you haven't been to the toilet for 23 hours. Not only that but I've had three cups of coffee today, four different flavour squashes, an orange juice and a can of 7up. Nobody is going to accuse me of making a half-hearted effort, that's for sure. That's if there was anyone around to see it!

'Where've you been?' It's Carrot, leaning against the wall. The end bit that is, not the bit where the action takes place.

'Sorry,' I say rather breathlessly, 'hill... toilet... difficult....'

'That's ok, you're only five minutes late. I was just getting a bit worried, that's all.'

Don't get worried about simple things, Carrot, save it for when we possibly, but hopefully not, need it.

'What you gonna do then?' asks Carrot.

'Pee!'

'With no witnesses?'

'Just you and your tape measure. You have got it haven't you?'

'Yeah,' he pulls it out of a pocket with a flourish. I think he's finally getting the hang of that jacket.

'Right, stand back.'

I take my coat off and place my wooden box on it. Carrot looks at the box, then me, and takes a step back.

'Here goes.' I undo my flies and go for it. My initial thoughts are of relief. Twenty-three hours of relief. Then, after about five seconds I start to concentrate. Brian's line is in sight.

'Go on Eddie!' shouts Carrot.

Brian's line is not a problem. I soar past it. Carrot cheers. I keep going.

'Well done, mate!' Carrot pats me on the back.

'Stand back; I haven't finished yet,' I cry. Carrot moves away again.

'But you don't need to go any further, you've broken the record. I'll vouch for you.' There's desperation in his voice.

'It's much more than that Carrot. Much more.'

My stream gets higher and higher until the box starts to glow on my jacket.

'Eddie, your wooden block is glowing. Look!'

I glance over my shoulder before concentrating once more on the job in hand.

'There,' I shout. 'I've done it!'

'Done what, Eddie, done what?' calls out Carrot frantically. 'You passed Brian's line ages ago.'

'Not Brian's line, Carrot. Five feet. I've passed five feet!'

'B... b... but what about this thing?' He points at my glowing box.

'Don't worry about that, just pass the tape measure.'

Carrot takes a wide berth around the box and passes me the tape measure.

'Hold that end steady, this is really important.'

'But why?' Carrot is now sounding as if he's met his pizza monster again. Maybe he has.

'Just hold it still.'

I measure it.

'Five feet exactly. I knew it; five feet.'

Carrot lets go of the tape as he hears my over-exuberant cries. It recoils in to its chrome casing and raps me on the knuckles on its way.

'Oops, sorry,' he says.

'Don't worry, I got up to five feet.' As I say this, I slap my hand against the wall as if to thank it for its part in the proceedings.

There's a pause.

The whole wall begins to shake. Nothing else, just the wall. The trees remain still, the ground remains still. The wall trembles.

The box is glowing, the wall is shaking. Then it all stops. No more glowing, no more shaking. Then, quite quietly, one brick falls out of the wall. It lands, much to our amazement, without making a sound. The hole left by the brick is three along to the left from my new record. Exactly five feet high.

'That was close,' says Carrot. 'For a moment there I thought the whole wall was gonna come down!'

'Yeah,' I whisper.

'Can we go now; it's getting a bit dark and I'm getting a bit cold.'

'In a minute. I just wanna look through the hole left by the falling brick.'

'Why?' says Carrot, edging down the hill. 'It's just the other side of the wall and the rest of the woods. You've seen it all before.'

'I won't be a sec.'

I stand on top of the fallen brick and stare through the hole. It's dark the other side. No trees, no sky, then it starts. It pulls me. The wall, something, starts to suck me. I resist, I fight back but it pulls. It doesn't hurt as such; it just pulls and sucks and pulls and pulls and.............

'Eddieeeeeee............'

# Chapter Three


'Welcome to my Realm.'

The voice is loud and booming. Echoing around the apparent void.

'I said; "Welcome to my Realm."'

I suddenly wish I was alongside Carrot, facing his pizza monster.

'H... h... hello!' I try to get the word out in one, so as not to sound frightened, but the stutter just h... h... happens. Oh no, I'm even stuttering in my thoughts. This place and that voice are obviously scaring me more than I thought they were. I try again.

'Hello.' That was better.

'Welcome to my....' The voice stops as it is interrupted by another.

'Will you stop that, Herf.'

'Why?' says the first voice again, sounding less booming than before.

''Coz you're frightening him.'

'I'm not frightened,' I call back.

'That's my boy,' says the second voice, as a sort of torch is lit about ten feet in front of me. 'He always said he would be brave.' He? Who's He?

I can now see that I'm in a room. Not a big room. It's about the size of our living room at home. There are two figures standing close to the flaming torch. One starts to move towards me. He stops just in front of me, smiling. At least I think it's a smile. It's difficult to tell because he has a light brown moustache hanging over his whole mouth. He's about my height, quite human-looking really. He's just a bit pale and in need of a shaver; or at least a trimmer.

'Hello, Eddie.' How does he know my name? 'I'm Medwick, and this is Herf.'

The other figure moves forward. He's very similar to the other one. Slightly shorter and with a black moustache desperately in need of a cut.

'Hello,' he says. His voice is no longer booming, although it is still a bit deeper than the others. 'Sorry if I scared you with my impression.'

'Impression? Of whom?'

'Be quiet, Herf. One thing at a time.'

'Sorry, Medwick.' Herf takes half a step back. I think I now know who's in charge.

'What are you, where am I and what's going on?' Three questions at once. That must show fear, mustn't it?

'I thought he's supposed to know everything already,' offers Herf.

'Herf!' Eye contact is exchanged.

'Sorry!' says Herf once more.

'Eddie does know everything. Well, almost everything. But He did tell us that it might take some time for it all to become clear.'

'He? Who is He? And how do you know my name?' That's five questions now. Do you think he's noticed?

'That's five questions now Eddie.' He's noticed. 'The answers to which will all be apparent very soon. The only thing you need to know at this time is that we are your friends.'

He takes my hand. Ah; I think I've noticed something else which is different between my new "friends" and my old. I look down at his hand.

'Sorry,' says Medwick. 'I should have mentioned my other thumb!'

His hand is "normal" except for the presence of another thumb directly opposite the thumb you would expect to find. Sort of down from his little finger.

'That's ok,' I say. 'Must be handy when faced with a stubborn jam jar lid!'

Herf and Medwick exchange glances again and smile.

'That's exactly what He said when we first met Him! You are definitely Eddie!'

I know I am, but I still don't know how they know.

'Are you going to answer any of my questions now?' I look expectantly at Medwick.

'Not just yet. Things aren't quite right.'

No. I've just been sucked through a gap in a wall the size of one brick and I'm now talking to two men with oversized moustaches and two thumbs on each hand. I suppose things aren't quite right!

'Do you still have the box?' searches Medwick. 'The carved wooden one.'

'Yes.'

'Where is it?'

'The other side of the wall.' I turn to see the wall. I'm pleased to see that the missing brick on my side is still missing on this side.

'You need to return to your world and return with it at this hour tomorrow.'

'Why?'

'I will answer that tomorrow.' Great.

Medwick continues.

'You need to bring some friends with you.'

'Friends? How many?'

'Herf!' Medwick calls to his companion.

Herf pulls an old looking scroll from his pocket, unrolls it and begins,

'"Eight or more is far too many, for the task ahead of you. Four or less is far too little, and it simply just won't do."' He rolls the scroll back up and replaces it in his pocket.

Medwick rolls his eyes.

'Herf said he wanted to do it properly,' he explains. 'All it means is that there must be five, six or seven of you to have any chance of success.'

Five, six or seven? There's me and Carrot, that's it!

'Ok.' Ok? What am I on about? I know one Carrot, not a bunch of them!

'What am I trying to succeed at?'

'All in good time, Eddie. All in good time.'

How did I know he was going to say that?

'Now you must return home and come back at this time tomorrow with your friends and the box. Do not forget the box Eddie. Do not forget the box.'

'Ok.' I keep saying ok as if everything is *cool* and I do this sort of thing all the time. What more can I say? He won't answer any of my questions until tomorrow, so "ok" is going to have to be it.

'How do I get back?'

'Just the same way as you got here,' says Medwick. 'Look through the gap in the wall and it will return you.'

'Ok,' I must think up a new catchphrase. "Ok" just isn't me. 'I'll see you tomorrow.' I try a smile.

'Bye Eddie,' calls out Herf.

'Until tomorrow, Master Eddie,' says Medwick, shaking my hand once more. 'Take care, boy, take care.'

I turn and look through the gap in the wall. Carrot is there, but I don't think he can see me. The wall pulls and sucks again, but it doesn't feel as strange or as uncomfortable as before, and then I'm through.

\*

'Carrot. Carrot!' I can't see him.

'Where did you go!?' He appears round the end of the wall. 'The wall sucked you in, but you didn't come out the other side.'

Carrot looks extremely, and quite rightly, uncomfortable.

'How long have I been gone?'

'Well,' Carrot thinks, 'I looked through the gap, it didn't try and suck me in, then I walked round the back and then you called out my name. About –' he looks at his watch '– six seconds.'

'Good.'

'Good? What's good about being sucked through a tiny gap in a wall and then reappearing six seconds later?'

Good question.

Well, it looks like my first accomplice is going to be told of his role. I just hope Carrot can take it.

'Come on,' I pick up my coat and box (which is no longer warm or glowing), 'I'll explain.'

We slowly walk down the hill as I try and fill Carrot in. The thing is, none of my questions were answered by Medwick or Herf, so it's even more difficult than I thought it would be.

*

'Adam; Karl; Jack; the two Darrens; Kev; Dave….'

'Whoa, Carrot!' Believe it or not, Carrot accepted my story! He said he would stand by my side "through thick and thin". I thought he would sleep on it and change his mind, but instead he's reeling off this list of possible accomplices as we stand together on the playground.

'When did you write this list?' I ask him.

'Last night, when I got in. I sat in bed thinking of everyone we knew.'

He seems a bit too excited to me. I tried to get across the gravity of the situation, the possible dangers of the situation, the complete *weirdness* of the situation, but, because I hadn't seen anything dangerous in "The Realm" I found it very difficult to do so. I think Carrot is thinking that our little trip through the wall is going to be like a Sunday morning drive. At the moment I don't know either way. It might be like that, but I doubt it.

'Do we know these people?' Carrot looks bemused.

''Course we do. Most are in our form and if they're not in our form they're in some of our classes.'

'Yes, I know that. But, do we really know them?' I think I've lost him now. 'These people are friends, but we don't really *know* them. We only see them in school. We don't go round anyone's house except each other's.'

'If that's the necessary requirement then we're stuffed!' He folds up the piece of paper with the list of names on it and puts it back into one of his pockets. The pocket probably has a name. I couldn't tell you.

'It's not a necessary requirement,' I say, 'I just think that the better we know them, the better we will get on and the easier it will be.'

'If you had found out what we were supposed to succeed at, this whole process would be much easier.'

Once more, Carrot is correct. I smile and shrug my shoulders.

'Who do we know well?'

Carrot thinks about my question.

'Besides each other, who do we know best?'

The extension of the original question hasn't really helped. We stand and think together.

'I don't know anyone,' says Carrot. 'You are the only person, besides my mum and dad, who I really know.'

That's sad. To be honest, I can't do much better.

'My sister!'

'Your sister? Is that the best you can do?'

'Well, it's one more than you!' Carrot looks down at his feet. 'Sorry, mate.'

'That's ok,' he looks up again, 'but really, your sister?'

'Well, I do know her well. I see a lot of her and we do get on quite well, for brother and sister.' Carrot thinks again. It's true, Liz and I do get on quite well. We bicker and squabble a bit, but compared to a lot of stories about siblings I think we are ok.

'I suppose she is ok for a sister; I wouldn't know.'

Carrot, if you hadn't already guessed, is a single child.

'That's three. Know anyone else?'

'Becky,' I say.

'Becky? Which Becky?'

'My sister's best friend, Becky.'

'Do you know her?'

Fair question.

'I mean *really* know her?'

Ok, Carrot, I get the point.

'No,' is my reply, 'but I see a lot of her and Liz knows her really well, probably as well as we know each other.'

This is true. Becky and Liz have been friends for as long as I can remember. Eight or nine years.

'I suppose it will make persuading Liz much easier, if we tell her that Becky can come as well.'

'Good idea, Carrot, I hadn't thought of that.' I had actually, but there's no harm in boosting Carrot's confidence before we enter The Realm, is there?

'We're still one short though,' says Carrot, 'any more suggestions?'

'Let's just hope that Liz and Becky agree and that we are only one short, and not three.'

\*

'Are you seeing Becky tonight?' The challenge begins.

'Yeah, why?'

'Just wondered.' Just wondered! What sort of an answer is that?

'You seeing Carrot?' Ah! A two-way conversation. I must build on this.

'Yes, why?'

'Just wondered!' She probably is just wondering and not trying to work out a way of inviting us on a trip into another place (or time, or whatever The Realm is). 'What are you getting up to tonight?'

I see an opportunity and seize it.

'We're going up the wall at eight. Wayne's gonna....' I stop, on purpose.

'Wayne's gonna what?'

'Nothing!'

She presses on.

'No, go on, finish off your sentence. Wayne's gonna what?'

Got you!

'Nothing... really.' I wander off upstairs.

Now, I know both my sister and Becky like Wayne. I just hope they like him enough to want to go up to the wall to see what *he's* doing up there!

*

'You there, Carrot?'

It's five to eight.

'Yeah, I'm here.' He pokes his head round from behind the wall. 'Where are Liz and Becky?'

'They're on their way.' I hope. Liz went round Becky's about an hour ago. I just hope that they decide on coming up to have a peek at Wayne!

'So, they agreed then? Just like that?'

'Not exactly,' I try not to look too worried. 'There isn't time to explain.' I usher Carrot back round behind the wall to wait for the girls to appear.

'Oi, you two!' Carrot and I turn with a start. 'What are you doing here?' Oh no, it's Brian. What the hell is *he* doing here.

'Nothing.' I say.

'It doesn't look like nothing; it looks like you're hiding.'

'No, just hanging loose,' says Carrot.

Hanging loose! What does that mean?

'Oh, cool,' says Brian, 'I often come up here to do that.' Oh, well, at least Brian knows what it means. 'I sometimes come up and check my mark is still on the wall as well.' Sad. 'Mind if I hang out with....'

'Ssh,' I interrupt, 'get down!'

Believe it or not, they do. Both of them! I can hear Liz and Becky coming up the hill.

'Who is it?' asks Brian.

'I don't know.' I do.

'Let's have a look,' Brian peers round the end of the wall. 'Oh, it's only your sister and Becky,' and off he strides to greet them!

25

'No, don't! Come back Brian!' I shout in the loudest whisper I know. But he's gone.

'What should we do?' says Carrot.

'I suppose we should go out as well,' I say reluctantly.

I lead, Carrot follows.

'Hi Sis!' I say in a bright and cheery fashion.

'Hello, what are you all doing behind there?'

'Hanging loose!' guffaws Brian. The girls just giggle.

'Actually, we're waiting for Wayne,' I retort.

'Are we?' says Carrot. Thanks mate!

'Yes, Carrot,' I laugh, 'you have a memory like a sieve.' I tap my head to demonstrate Carrot's stupidity. He just looks at me, bemused.

'I've never seen Wayne up here,' joins in Brian. This is not going at all to plan.

'I tell you what,' I say whilst glancing at my watch and realising it's one minute to eight, 'why don't I show you a trick I practised up here at the wall last night?' I decide to take my chance and try and get my unknowing accomplices through the wall.

'We're not interested in tricks, are we Becky?' says Liz.

'No, we just wanna see Wayne!' They both giggle again. I can see I'm going to have trouble with all of their giggling.

'No,' says Carrot, 'you'll like this trick, it's really impressive!' Attaboy Carrot, we're now on the same wavelength as each other.

'What you gonna do then?' says Brian. 'You ain't gonna pee up the wall are ya? It won't count you know. Not with girls watching!'

Oh, Brian. How can you be part of my team? Sixty million people in the country and I get Brian. Number sixty million and one.

'No, Brian. I am not going to do that. I'm going to pass through that gap in the wall.' I say this in a "you won't believe it" voice as I point up to the hole left by the brick.

'Don't be silly, Eddie,' says my sister. 'If Wayne isn't gonna turn up, we're going home.'

Becky glances at her watch.

'Yeah, it's just gone eight,' she says, 'we'd better go.'

'Just let me have one shot at it, that's all I ask.' Desperation is creeping in to my voice.

'Eddie, you are a boy. Not a big boy,' Becky giggles again, she's worse than my sister for giggling so it would seem, 'but a boy all the same and you are not, I repeat not, going to fit through a gap that is the size of one brick!'

'When did that brick fall out?' Oh Brian, do please keep up. We all ignore him.

'I tell you what, if I look like I'm gonna get stuck you'll pull me back, won't you Sis?'

The girls *and* Brian giggle. Well, the girls giggle, Brian guffaws.

'Just say you will.' I'm now clearly pleading with her.

Liz stares at me, I think she can sense something's wrong.

'You alright Eddie?'

'Yes, just promise you will take my hand if I get stuck.' The giggling has stopped.

'Ok,' says Liz in a much more caring "big sister" style, 'if that's what you want.'

'And will you take Liz's hand if she gets stuck please Becky?'

'What?' says Becky.

'And Brian, will you take Becky's hand if she gets stuck? And you Brian's, Carrot?'

There is silence. Maybe I've gone too far.

'Why don't we all say yes,' says Liz, 'let Eddie try his silly trick and then we can all go home, ok?'

'Ok,' says Becky, 'if it keeps you happy!'

I smile.

'Of course,' says Carrot.

'I'm not having Carrot grab hold of my hand. Can't I go in between the two girls?'

Brian grins an unattractive grin and drools ever so slightly.

'It's not gonna come to that, is it Brian? So just say yes!' My sister is firm. I think Brian likes that.

'Ok,' is his reply.

'Right,' I say in my best magician's voice, 'here goes!'

I look through the hole. The sucking and pulling begins. I quickly put a hand behind me so that Liz can get hold of me.

'Eddie, what's happening?' I hear my sister's voice.

'It's ok, says Carrot, it's all part of the trick!' Carrot's voice becomes distant as I am sucked through the hole.

'Eddieeeee.' It's my sister's voice, very faint. I feel her grab my hand at the last second as I'm pulled through. I just hope all the others did as they promised they would.

# Chapter Four

It's dark.

Very dark.

In fact, the only time I've seen darkness like this, if you can *see* darkness, was when we all turned our lamps off on a school potholing trip last year. Two hundred feet below ground. Black.

I feel a tug on my left hand.

'Eddie, what's happened, Eddie...?'

It's my sister and I've never heard anyone sound so scared in my whole life.

'It's ok,' I tighten my grip to try and reassure her, 'they'll put a light on in a few seconds.'

'They? Who are they?' The first of many questions, I fear.

'Ssh!' I say as the torch is lit as before.

'Five,' says the voice of a figure near the torch. I think it's Medwick.

'That's the minimum!' That's Herf.

I turn to check that there are five of us. Becky and Carrot look as frightened as Liz. In between them is a petrified Brian who is squeezing both Becky's and Carrot's hands far too tight.

'Can you let go now Brian?' asks Becky. Brian just stares ahead at the torch. Speechless. 'Brian!!'

Brian, without a word, lets go of them. Becky and Carrot turn their troubled stares towards me and Brian continues to gaze at the torch. Great. The big, tough one we bring is the most scared. Brilliant!

Another torch is lit. Medwick and Herf approach.

'Eddie,' says Medwick taking my hand. 'I knew you would return.' I return his smile. 'Your friends look a bit more frightened of their surroundings than I had anticipated.'

I turn and look at my counterparts. They are a sorry bunch.

'Hello, I'm Carrot. You must be Medwick?'

Thank you, Carrot.

'Indeed, I am, young Master Carrot. And you must be Eddie's best friend?'

'I am. How did you know that?'

'Because,' continues Medwick, 'I get the feeling you are the only one who knows my name!'

There's a silence.

'He is,' I say. 'The others weren't made aware of you, or any of this.'

I wave my arm around the room.

'Did you trick them, Eddie?' asks Medwick.

I look at the floor. 'Yes…. Sorry.'

'Don't be sorry. You may require a lot of trickery while you are here. There's no harm in a bit of practice, is there!?' He smiles another of his moustache-covered smiles. 'I think that you need to bring your friends up to date, don't you?'

'Ok, but I don't know much, do I?'

'You tell them as much as you know, then Herf and I will answer all your questions, won't we Herf?'

'Yes, we will!' Herf sounds quite excited that he's being included in this.

'We shall get you something to eat and drink whilst you explain.'

Medwick walks away, closely followed by Herf. As I turn around, with Carrot by my side, I feel very aware of three pairs of eyes burning in to me, waiting for my explanation.

*

'Do your friends all understand now?' asks Medwick, once I've finished my story and made all the introductions.

'We understand that we are in The Realm, wherever that is, that Eddie's box is important and that you have two thumbs! Not much of an explanation really!' Liz isn't too impressed. Brian and Becky just listened to my explanation. Liz, probably because she's my big sister, just moaned and grumbled.

We are all sitting around a table covered with quite a lot of food and drink.

'Shall I try and pre-empt all of your questions by just telling you everything from the beginning?'

Everyone looks at me, so I suppose it should be me who answers.

'Ok,' I say. Oh no, not the "Ok's" again.

'Right then,' continues Medwick, 'eat and drink, but try not to interrupt. Hopefully any questions you currently have in your mind will be answered at some point during the following.'

He sips his drink. Or at least I think he's sipping his drink. All I can see is his moustache dipping in and out of the cup. If it's the same drink as mine it's a sort of fruit flavour, a bit like mango.

'Almost eleven years ago, in fact eleven years ago next Wednesday —' next Wednesday? That's my twelfth birthday! '— a man appeared in this room, just like Eddie and the rest of you have done. He came through that door there,' he points to a wooden door, 'not through the gap in the wall like you. We believe that the wall you entered through is all that now remains of this building. Is that right, Eddie?'

'Yes,' I say, 'it is.'

'Eleven years ago, this whole building was a portal between our two realms.'

'What's a portal?' whispers Brian.

'Herf, answer him!' says Medwick.

'Yes Medwick,' replies Herf. 'A portal is a link between two places; a gateway between your World and our Realm.'

'Thank you Herf.' He glares at Big Brian. 'And please try not to interrupt again or we'll be here all night!'

'Sorry,' whispers Brian. An apology from Brian. He must be nervous!

'Eleven years ago, this building was quite a normal looking building in your world. Just derelict. The majority of it was destroyed more recently by a storm, leaving the wall as the only remaining link between our two realms. The man had walked in to this building expecting it to be derelict, as it appeared to be in that state in your world, but he came across me.' Medwick pauses and gives his moustache another bath in his drink. We all look at each other, expectantly. 'As you can see,' he continues, 'this building is not derelict in this realm, it is my home. The reason the man could enter my home, and indeed this realm, was because he belonged here.'

We're all now clearly desperate to throw questions at Medwick such as; who's this man? Why does he belong here? What are we doing here? But we all refrain and wait, hoping that it will all become clear.

'This man's great, great grandfather had once been the ruler of The Realm. He lost a huge battle against another, lost his throne and his descendants were lost, thrown to the far reaches of The Realm. The man who entered my home eleven years ago was the first descendant to find his way back to The Realm. It had taken one hundred and three years for the rightful heir to return.' One hundred and three? How old is Medwick then? 'You are probably wondering who the man was, aren't you?' We all stare at Medwick. I'm holding my breath. 'Eddie; he was your uncle.'

*Major* pause. In fact; **MAJOR** pause!

It's Liz who breaks the silence. 'Uncle Mark?'

Herf bows at the sound of the name.

'Yes, that's right, your uncle as well.'

'Didn't he die?' I say.

'No,' says Liz who was three at the time. I was nearly one. 'He just disappeared.'

'Disappeared? No one told me!'

'Nothing to tell really. He just disappeared. Or so we thought.' Nothing to tell! Huh!

'He did disappear from your world. He came here. He returned to take his rightful place as the Ruler of The Realm.'

Hang on. I can see him now. Holding me. Should I be able to remember that? I wasn't even one year old.

'Are you ok, Eddie?' asks Medwick. 'You look troubled.'

'I don't know what's happening, but I can remember things. Things to do with Uncle Mark.'

'He's remembering,' cries out Herf with glee. 'I knew he would!'

'What else Eddie? What else can you remember?' Medwick is urging me on.

'He left me the box on my birthday and said he would see me again one day.'

'That's it! That's it!' Herf is jumping around the table.

'Please calm down, Herf, this is just the beginning,' says Medwick, remaining quite calm.

'So, where is he, can we see him?'

'Yes, can we see him?' joins in Liz.

'Allow me to continue and your questions will be answered,' says Medwick.

We settle down for the resumption of the story.

'The day your uncle arrived I knew who he was. The resemblance to his great, great grandfather was amazing. He stood in that doorway, with the sun behind him. He was blinking to try and get his eyes used to the dim room. I don't think his eyes had really adjusted, as when he first saw me, sitting in this chair, he thought I was a homeless old man in need of help! Because he was such a caring young man he didn't turn and leave but came and knelt beside me.'

Medwick pauses as if lost in the memory.

'Then what happened?' asks Liz who, like us all, is engrossed in the story.

'Well,' continues Medwick, 'as your uncle became used to the light, he realised that I wasn't quite human. He sat on the floor, even though I'd offered him my chair, and allowed me to tell him the story of The Realm.'

'How did he take that?' I ask.

'He said,' replies Medwick, 'that he'd always thought that there was more to life than life. That there was more to living than living and that there was more to the Earth than earth.'

My friends all look rather confused. As am I?

'What does that mean?' blurts out Brian, breaking the silence.

'Herf!' says Medwick.

33

'It means,' replies Herf, 'that those humans who have a connection with The Realm will have a need to search for *more* until that connection is hopefully made.'

I think I get it. Although Brian still looks confused!

'I told your uncle,' continues Medwick, 'that if anything ever happened to him, I did not want to wait for another 103 years for another descendant to hopefully find the connection. I wanted to place a trigger, on Earth. So, I gave him the box, which I hope you have with you.' I remove it from inside my coat and place it in the middle of the table. 'And I told him to give it to his next of kin before returning for good. He gave it to you Eddie.'

'Why did he give it to you, Eddie?' inquires Carrot.

'I don't know,' I say.

'Uncle Mark never married,' says Liz, 'and you are his little sister's, our mum's, only son. So, I suppose being his nephew makes you his nearest male next of kin. Is that right Medwick?'

'That is correct. For the few years before your brother was born, you were the next of kin, but our Ruler is like a lot of royal families; males come first if at all possible.'

'So, can we see him now?' I say.

'The box,' says Medwick, 'will only call you when you're needed by The Realm. Ten years ago, your uncle's attempt to reclaim his throne failed. You are now needed by The Realm.'

'If it failed ten years ago, why didn't it call me then?' I ask.

'You would have only been two years old, Eddie. Not a lot of use I feel!'

Becky giggles. Medwick frowns at her.

'Sorry,' Becky says.

'What must I do? Help Uncle Mark reclaim his throne?' I say.

'The being that overthrew your great, great, great grandfather is the same one that put down your uncle's attempts to reclaim his throne.' Being? I don't like the sound of that. 'He decided not to banish your uncle, as he had done with his predecessor, in case he returned to challenge him again. Instead, he imprisoned him. You must lead the challenge to rescue him and return him to the throne.'

I swallow, visibly and very loudly.

'How can we take on a "being" that's overthrown one Ruler, stopped another and been on the throne for 114 years?'

Good question Carrot. If I could speak at this precise moment, I would have asked that.

'By using something that has not been in our realm for 114 years: your youth.'

'Our youth?' questions Liz.

'One hundred and fourteen years ago, the new leader forced everyone to take a drug that meant they could not have any more children. You are the youngest in The Realm by more than a century.'

'Doesn't that mean your race will die out?' says Becky.

'Eventually. Our race, the Gingoiles, live for about 250 years. I am 217.'

'And I'm 184,' joins in Herf.

'Their race live to over 400. Once we have all died, he will reverse the effect of the drug in his race and his people will rule The Realm. It's his way of destroying the Gingoiles without losing any of his race in any kind of conflict.'

'That's sad,' says Brian. He is *so* right.

'How can he reverse the effect of the drug?' I have now regained my voice.

'He has the formula locked away. Locked away in an even more secure place than your uncle.' Oh.

'So, we use our youth, do we?' I say.

'Yes, Eddie. It is something they only know about from times past,' says Medwick, 'therefore they might have some kind of weakness if they lack knowledge about youth.'

'So that's why the box called Eddie when he's almost 12?' asks Carrot, 'and not, say, when he's 18 or 20?'

'That's right,' replies Medwick.

'How did it know I was almost 12?' I ask.

'Herf, do you wish to explain this one?' says Medwick.

'I do,' says Herf. He clearly loves being asked to help. 'Your uncle wanted you to be the right age. Wise, but young. He didn't think he would need you, because he thought he would get his throne back, but if he did need you, he wanted you to be about 12 years old. He thought this would give the correct balance between age and wisdom.' He sips his drink. He has the same problem with his moustache as Medwick. 'Your uncle remembered erm... erm...'

'Come on Herf, spit it out!' says Medwick.

'Your uncle remembered,' Herf coughs, 'urinating up the outside of that wall as a child.'

'Urinating? What's that?' I hear Brian quietly ask of Carrot.

'Peeing,' whispers Carrot under his breath. Brian understands that word.

'He remembers beating every other child in his school in a competition. He says he reached five feet up the wall.'

'Five feet,' asks Brian in a louder voice, 'how high is that?'

It's amazing isn't it? Here we are in another world and Brian still seems to show more interest in his peeing record.

'One metre 52 and a half centimetres,' I say.

'I thought my 1 metre 45 was the record?'

'Exactly,' cries Herf, 'Eddie's uncle knew that his five feet was something extraordinary and that no one, however big,' he looks up and down at the size of Brian, 'would beat it. The box was designed to make you want to,' he coughs again, 'urinate up the wall to five feet so as to find the portal.'

'But he's never peed that high!' says Brian.

'He has,' says Carrot, 'last night. How do you think we got here?'

Brian sits and thinks. We wait for his reply.

'Ok, fair enough,' he says, 'but it won't count as the record you know. Not enough witnesses!'

'Oh, do be quiet, Brian.' Liz is firm with him again.

'Your uncle,' continues Herf, 'remembers being 12 when he reached five feet. That's why he thought up this way of you finding the portal.'

'And,' Medwick takes over,' seeing as you are not 12 for another six days, it seems that you have surpassed your uncle!'

I feel quite proud.

'And what is this other race called?' I ask. Well, I need to know, don't I?

'They are the Thargs, and their leader and The Ruler of The Realm, is the ruthless Zendorf.'

We all seem to shiver as one.

'Do they look like you?' asks Becky.

'No,' replies Medwick. 'Although we were all one race hundreds of thousands of years ago, we developed differently. The Thargs are taller than us, but no taller than Brian.' Brian smiles, his size might just come in handy. 'They do not have moustaches, but they have protruding cheekbones.' He points to his face to demonstrate this. 'They are pale, like us, and what you would call their second thumb is more finger-like.'

'Are there many of them?' I ask.

'We, the Gingoiles, still outnumber them, but without the formula to reverse the effect of the drug, they will soon outnumber us. They are also physically stronger than us.'

'Can't you beat them mentally?' asks Carrot.

'Indeed, we can, but they know our ways and can counteract them using force. We cannot allow our numbers to dwindle any more. The Thargs do not know your way. The minds of the young.'

'I'm not sure that our youth is going to count for much, Medwick,' I say. We might have a child-like approach, which might surprise them, but I can't see Zendorf being surprised out of rulership, can you?

'Sleep on it, Eddie,' says Medwick, 'you will come up with some ideas. We can talk more in the morning.'

'Sleep!' cries Becky. 'Don't you think our parents are going to miss us if we stay here all night?' Good point.

'When you return to your world the time will be the same as when you came here. Your parents will not miss you at all!'

'How come, when Eddie came here last night, it took six seconds for him to reappear?' Asks Carrot. Another good point.

'That was the storm,' replies Herf. 'The storm that destroyed the building in your world put us out of alignment by six seconds. That's why you sort of get sucked through, instead of just coming through. It's to compensate for the time difference. Whatever you do here will only last six seconds in your world.'

37

We all look at each other trying to grasp the physics of it all. I wonder what Mr Pearson, our science teacher, would make of all this?

'Right,' says Medwick, getting to his feet, 'that's enough for one day. Let me take you to your rooms. You all need some sleep.'

We all know he's right, but I'm not sure any of us are going to get much sleep tonight.

'Just one moment, Medwick,' says Liz as I'm just starting towards the door. 'If everything we do here only lasts six seconds in our world, how come we all thought Uncle Mark had disappeared?'

Now that is a good question!

'Because he's meant to be here, Liz,' comes Medwick's reply.

'Isn't Eddie meant to be here?' continues Liz. 'Seeing as he's the next Ruler isn't he meant to be here and therefore missed in our world?'

All eyes return to Medwick.

'As long as your uncle is alive, only six seconds will pass for all of you, including Eddie,' he replies, 'but if, and when, Eddie becomes Ruler, time will pass equally in both The Realm and your world. It will be at that point that Eddie will have to lead a double life. Something your uncle was briefly doing successfully until he was captured and was unable to return to your world and continue the life he led there.'

We all share puzzled glances.

'Right,' continues Medwick, 'now that's definitely enough for one day.'

# Chapter Five

Sleep! I wish. Carrot and I talked for ages. Brian didn't say much, except for constantly repeating that he was bigger than both the Gingoiles *and* the Thargs. Come to think of it, if we had counted the times Brian mentioned being six feet tall instead of counting sheep, we might have actually nodded off! Once Brian had shut up, Carrot and I began to discuss the issues facing us. Then, after only five minutes of this, Brian began to snore. And boy, could he snore! In between breaths Carrot and I decided upon a few things that we would take to the girls, Medwick and Herf in the morning.

*

'Right,' I say, trying to sound authoritative. After all, I am the nephew of the rightful ruler of a realm. 'We need to rescue Uncle Mark first, and then rescue the formula that will reverse the effect of the drug.' Impressive. My first decision made and announced.

'Well done, Einstein. Did it take you all night to work that one out?' Sisters, eh? They can be *so* cutting.

'No,' I retort, 'but I thought I would make it clear to *all* concerned.' I make a slight nod of my head in the direction of Brian. Liz smiles in recognition. 'As for how we are going to achieve these objectives, I'm not sure until I know where we have to go to be able to do the rescuing!' I look towards Medwick.

'You need a map, young Eddie,' says Medwick pointing to the box. 'You've had one all the time!'

'What,' I say, 'in the box?'

'But it hasn't got a lid,' joins in Carrot.

'It has in The Realm,' says Medwick, 'take a look.'

I pick it up and, well, my solid box has a lid which slides off in my hand, and there, inside, is a small folded up piece of paper. I open it up and lay it down on the table. It's a very simple map.

'Wow!' says Carrot. We're all thinking the same, but Carrot's expression of the word is enough for all of us.

'You also have the carvings on the outside of the box,' says Medwick, 'which are representations of landmarks you should come across on your way to The Dark Castle.'

'The Dark Castle,' says Becky with a shiver, 'that doesn't sound like the right name for a place where a ruler should live.'

'It's the right name, but the wrong place!' replies Medwick.

We all look like Brian, that is, confused!

'Can you explain, please Herf?'

Herf looks like he's been asked to play the leading role in a musical as he shuffles forward to take his own imaginary centre stage. He does get excited when Medwick asks for his assistance.

'The Ruler of The Realm's ancestral home' he begins, 'is The Palace of the Realm. A beautiful, white-walled building with marvellous gardens and….'

'Herf!' calls out Medwick, 'just the facts please!!'

'Sorry Medwick.' Liz and Becky giggle. 'It's really nice,' mutters Herf under his breath, 'too nice for Zendorf,' he says with a certain amount of venom that I hadn't noticed coming from the direction of Herf up until now. 'So after a couple of years he moved back to his own castle, which is really dirty. That's why we call it The Dark Castle, and The Palace of The Realm has been left empty ever since.'

'It's been empty for over one hundred years?' says Becky.

'Yes,' replies Herf.

'It must be completely dilapidated if no one's been living in it for that length of time?' continues Becky.

'Dilapi… what?' asks Brian.

'Dilapidated,' says Carrot trying to help him out, 'it means like a ruin.'

'Right.' By George he's got it!

'No one's living in it,' says Herf, 'that's not to say that no one's looking after it!'

'That's right,' continues Medwick. 'For over a century now, Gingoiles have looked after The Palace of The Realm. They have made all repairs and kept it clean and tidy so that as soon as the rightful ruler is returned, they can take up residence immediately.'

'Don't the Thargs try and stop you from looking after it?' I ask.

'They laugh at us, saying that we are wasting our time and that it will never be used again. But they let us continue, knowing that if a number of us are there, then we can't be elsewhere attacking them or trying to rescue your uncle.'

'It would be nice to see it,' says Liz.

'You shall,' replies Medwick. 'The Palace is halfway between here and The Dark Castle. You can rest there a few days.'

'I thought that only the Ruler could stay there?' says Carrot.

'And his descendant and his friends!' Medwick smiles at me as he speaks.

'How long will it take to get to the Palace?' asks Liz.

'A week,' says Medwick.

'And that's only halfway?' says Carrot.

'Approximately!'

'Then we should begin,' I say whilst looking at the map. 'Are we here?' I ask of Medwick.

'Yes, well worked out young Eddie.'

'And we're trying to get to here?'

'Correct again,' says Medwick.

'And where's the Palace?'

'It's there, isn't it?' says Carrot.

'Well done, Carrot!' Carrot beams. 'With you two in charge of directions I'm sure you won't get lost!'

'If it's going to take a week to get to the Palace, where are we supposed to sleep each night *before* we get there?' Good question Liz.

'There are Gingoiles around who are aware of your presence. They will help,' says Medwick, 'but we are trying not to arouse the Thargs' suspicions, so you may have to fend for yourselves some nights.'

My team of Thargbusters is beginning to look a bit scared!

'You mean we may come across Thargs before we reach The Dark Castle?' asks Becky.

'Oh yes,' says Medwick, 'I'm afraid that they are everywhere.'

'I was hoping that we wouldn't encounter them until we were inside the castle walls,' says Becky.

'They are concentrated more highly near to the castle, but they could be anywhere, even outside my front door!'

Carrot glances over his shoulder to check that there isn't a Tharg looking through the window at him. My team now looks beyond scared.

'Herf has sorted out some provisions for you,' Medwick points to five knapsacks in the corner of the room. 'Any Gingoile you meet will offer you food, so don't worry about your stomachs!'

'Aren't either of you coming with us?' I look at Medwick and Herf in turn. I know that they are not, but I have to ask, don't I?

'That would raise too much suspicion, Eddie.' I told you, didn't I? 'You must achieve this by yourselves.' Great.

*

We line up with our knapsacks on our backs. I don't think that we'll be doing too much val-de-ree or val-de-ra whilst we are in possession of them.

'Now,' says Medwick firmly. 'The possible routes are marked on the map. Each is as difficult as the next.'

'Difficult? In what way?' asks Carrot.

'Herf!' calls Medwick.

'It's usually the terrain,' begins Herf.

Carrot mutters "the ground" to Brian before he can ask what the word terrain means.

'And this can vary depending upon the weather.'

'What's the weather usually like at this time of year?' I ask.

'I'm afraid that the weather in The Realm does not conform to any kind of seasons that you are used to. It just happens!' says Herf. 'That's why we cannot suggest one route over another. In a flash the weather can change and make the good route the bad and vice versa!'

Where's a weather reporter when you need one?

'So,' says Liz, 'besides the Thargs, the terrain and the changeable weather, there's nothing else to worry about?'

There is a hint of sarcasm in this.

'No, that's just about it,' says Herf completely unconvincingly.

'Just about?' joins in Becky.

Medwick takes over.

'Other things are even harder to predict than the weather. With a bit of luck, you will only see sun, clear paths and no Thargs. I could tell you of other possible dangers, but why worry you when they may not arise?'

I'm not sure that telling us that there *are* possible dangers, but not telling us *what* they are, is particularly comforting!

'Just try and follow the general routes without sticking to them religiously. There is usually plenty of cover either side of the paths.' Now, that is good advice. 'And use the box as a guide. The carvings will help. Trust me.' I tap my pocket to check the box is still with me. It is.

'Right!' I say, trying not to sound too excited, 'off we go!'

'Bye, Eddie,' says Herf.

'Good luck, Master Eddie,' says Medwick. 'We shall be with you in spirit, always.' He gives me the broadest grin I have seen him give. 'Best wishes to you all!'

Carrot joins in the parting by shaking both the Gingoiles' hands. Becky and Brian do likewise. Liz gives them both a hug. I'm sure Herf doesn't look quite as pale as normal. I think the embarrassment has turned him a tad red!

I walk out into the sunlight. It's the first time we've seen the outdoors of The Realm. The others all stop beside me as we look around. It is bright and green. We are in the countryside of a beautiful place.

'It's beautiful,' says Becky. I'm clearly not alone in my summing-up of the place.

'A place as pleasant as this needs to be ruled by the rightful, good ruler,' I say. I think I'm getting into this role of leader and morale-booster already. 'This is no place for evil to reside!' I think I'll stop there for the moment. Any more and I might just strike a Churchill-like pose I saw on a World War Two poster in a history lesson.

'It reminds me of the lakes and hills and white-topped mountains I saw in Austria,' reminisces Carrot.

'I think it's like that place we visited in the South of France,' says my sister, 'do you remember that place Eddie?'

'Yes,' I reply, 'it does have similarities.'

'It reminds me of parts of New Zealand,' says Becky. 'I went there a couple of years ago.'

There's a pause as we all wonder at the beauty.

'Yorkshire!'

We all turn and look at Brian.

'It reminds me of Yorkshire!' repeats our larger companion.

I almost say, "you don't get out much" but I refrain. I'm not sure about the snow-peaked mountains though!

We all turn our gaze back to our surroundings. Then I hear a cough. It's Medwick, standing in his doorway behind us.

'Try to not look too conspicuous!' he says, referring to the fact that there are five humans standing in the open, looking around, open-mouthed, in a world that is not their own!

'Whoops!' I say, as I wave to Medwick and hurry the others in to the trees and bushes that are next to the road.

'What first?' asks Carrot.

'We'll take this low road,' I say pointing to the map. 'We can try and stay in the cover between this road –' I point at the line on the map representing the road that we are currently standing next to '– and this ridge of mountains.'

'What about when we get to this fork in the road?' asks Liz. 'Do we go up the mountainside or down towards the river in the valley?'

I peer at the map.

'I think we should try the valley, then maybe we can reach this village –' I point once more at the map '– and spend the night with some Gingoiles. Ok?'

'Ok,' say Liz and Becky. Brian and Carrot both nod in agreement.

'Hang on,' I say as I retrieve the box from my pocket. 'I can feel this giving off some heat.'

I hold the box out for all to see.

'Is that good or bad?' asks my sis.

'I don't know,' I reply. 'Good, I think. Well; I'm pretty sure it's glowed and given off heat at positive times.'

'Did it just start getting warm when we were discussing the route?' asks Becky.

'Yes,' I reply, 'when we were discussing which direction to take at the fork in the road.'

'Try it again,' says Becky.

'Try what?' I answer.

'Talk about whether to take the mountain or valley route.'

'Oh, ok,' I say. 'When we get to the fork in the road should we go up the mountainside?' I pause to give the box a chance to warm-up. It doesn't. 'Or the valley?' I pause again. Heat! 'It's warming up!' I say.

Everyone leans in and touches the box before the gentle warmth subsides.

'Definitely some warmth,' says Liz.

'Yes,' reply the others.

'So,' I say, 'the box is some sort of guide, or compass, as well as a map-holder?'

'And Medwick said that the carvings around the edge are important,' adds Brian.

'You're right, Brian,' I say. 'He did say that.'

We all marvel at the box which I eventually put back in my pocket.

'Let's just hope that heat is good,' says Carrot, 'and not bad!'

'I guess we'll find out in the village,' replies Liz.

'I guess so,' I add.

There seems to be a pause as we all take things in.

'Right,' asks Carrot. 'Who's taking point?'

'Taking what?' I reply.

'Sorry, I mean going at the front?' Oh, I see. "Taking point." It's Carrot's commando-style jacket talking again.

'I don't mind,' I say, 'as long as we keep down and keep our eyes peeled.'

'Ok,' says Carrot. 'I'll take point. Brian –' he looks towards him '– you cover the rear and you girls stay close to Eddie in the middle. We must protect him at all costs!'

Everybody stares at Carrot.

Silence.

'What?' he says.

"What!" What does he mean, "What?"

'What?' says Liz, 'What do you mean, "What!"?'

That's what I just thought!

'I mean, what's wrong with the format?' continues Carrot.

'There's nothing wrong with the format,' replies my sister, 'it's the way you said it! All this "protect Eddie at all costs" stuff.'

'Well,' says Carrot, 'we *have* got to protect him at all costs.'

They all look at me. Have they got to protect me at all costs? I'm their leader because it's me who got them here and I am heir to the throne of The Realm, but if something happens to me, they can still succeed, can't they?

'Why do we have to protect him?' Becky joins in.

'Yeah, why?' adds Brian.

'We're here to rescue Mark and the antidote,' continues Becky. 'We will obviously try and achieve this with Eddie, but we will also try and achieve this without him if we have to!'

I hope that they don't need to do it without me, but at least they sound like they're up for it!

Carrot sighs.

'Eddie is the heir. If we rescue Mark then true; it doesn't matter too much about Eddie.' Thanks mate! 'But we could get all the way in to The Dark Castle and find that Zendorf has, well, got rid of Mark already, which means that Eddie isn't the heir, but the Ruler.'

Heavy stuff. I'd constantly been thinking about Mark being the ruler and me just coming to help, but I could actually end up ruling this place. In fact, I will eventually. Won't I? Well... probably.... All eyes are on me.

'I'm sure Uncle Mark is fine. But I suppose Carrot is right.'

'It makes sense to me,' says Liz. 'I'll protect you little bro.' She gives me a wink.

'We all will, Eddie,' says Becky. 'Won't we Brian?'

Brian smiles. A strange thing to see, a smiling Brian!

'Sure will. I'll be right behind you, covering your rear!'

The girls giggle at Brian. Carrot and I exchange smiles.

So here we are, I'm the leader, but Carrot is *actually* leading. I'm also here to protect the future of The Realm, whilst being protected by my companions.

It's a funny old Realm!

Chapter Six

Two hours we've been walking. Two hours under cover of some rather prickly trees and bushes. Becky cut herself ten minutes into our quest. Only a small cut on her hand. It did give Carrot the opportunity to produce a plaster from one of his pockets, though. It also gave Brian the opportunity to comfort Becky. You know; arm round the shoulder, drool on the chin (his chin, not Becky's)! Becky seemed extremely relieved with the speed Carrot produced the plaster. It was nothing to do with pain relief, well it was, but not pain relief from the finger, just the pain relief from being released from the grip of Brian!

We obviously haven't spoken much during this time, what with trying to not be too conspicuous! I don't know about the others, but I've been using the time to think. I've been thinking about a lot of things. I've been thinking that Brian likes Becky. Particularly since the cut hand incident. I mean, I quite like Becky, as a friend, but I get the impression Brian *really* likes her. I do wish he wouldn't drool, though. It's not a good look! I hope, when I *really* start to like girls, that I don't drool. At the moment I have no interest in going down that path. I don't even know if Becky's pretty. What's pretty anyway? Is blonde hair particularly pretty? Maybe. It's certainly different to the brown-haired Ross family!

Apart from hair colour I've been thinking about my Uncle Mark. The Realm. My friends. The route. The enormity of the task. The absurdity of the task. The Gingoiles. The Thargs. My mum's shepherd's pie... Well, I did say that I've been thinking about a lot of things!

'We're coming up to the fork in the road,' says Carrot. 'Are we still going to go down into the valley?'

'I can't see any reason to change our plans, can anyone else?' I look around. I feel that I should try and include my companions in as many decisions as possible. There are two reasons for this. Firstly, there is no real reason why I should be better at leading or taking control of our party than any other member of it. I mean a problem shared is a problem halved, or in my case a problem fifthed! Five heads are better than one, and all that. Secondly, I have absolutely no idea what I'm doing! I often struggle to stay in control of my remote-controlled car!

'No reason to change,' says Liz. 'We need to test our theory about the box warming up, anyway!'

Carrot and Becky nod in agreement. Brian shrugs his shoulders in a "makes no difference to me" kind of way.

'Going down the valley does look a bit easier than going up the mountainside,' says Carrot, 'but that means crossing the road before we can get back under the cover of the trees.'

'Ok,' I say, 'everyone look around really carefully to check that the coast is clear.'

I look around, as do the others. It is truly a magnificent place. And, at the moment, empty of any other beings!

'Nothing, Bruv,' says Liz.

'I can't see anything either,' says Becky.

I nod towards Carrot. He understands.

'Ok, let's go!' says our man at point. We edge forward towards the clearing that is the fork in the road.

'Hang on!' calls a loud, strained whisper. We all jump with fright. The four of us landing from jumping as one makes more noise than the voice. It's Brian.

'What's up?' I say to the hoarse whisperer.

'You never asked me!' he says.

'Never asked you what?'

'Whether I could see anything.'

Do you know; he's stood at the back, nodding or shaking his head in agreement with everything put forward. I'm sure he has perfected shrugging in the last two hours. Now he wants me to ask his opinion.

'Ok, Brian, do you think the coast is clear?'

He looks around.

'I'm not sure' is his belated reply. The others turn around to look at Brian. I stop looking at Brian and look across the road and up into the trees where Brian's eyes seem to be fixed.

'What do you think you can see?' I say as I gaze in to the trees. I can't see a thing!

'Up there,' Brian says, pointing with eyes so as to keep himself as still as possible. I try and follow his line of vision. I can still only see trees.

'Whereabouts?' I whisper.

'You see that big tree?' continues Brian.

They all look big to me, so I'll assume he means the biggest.

'Yes.'

'Two trees along to the left. About five metres up. There!'

I look. Two trees to the left and just over sixteen feet up and... yes, I can see something! I'm not sure what, but something is trying to stay out of sight.

'What do you think it is, Brian?'

He saw it first, maybe he has more idea than me!

'A Gingoile,' he replies.

I look again.

'Really!' I say. 'Are you sure?'

'Yep!' he says.

I look to the others.

'What do you lot think?' They all peer and squint into the trees.

'Can't see a thing!' says Liz.

'Nor me,' adds Carrot.

'I'm not sure,' says Becky. 'I think I can see something, but there is no way I can tell whether it's a Gingoile, a Tharg or anything else.'

Anything else? I don't remember Medwick or Herf mentioning "anything else"!

'Ok,' I say, 'three of us can see something, two of us can't; therefore, we must assume something is up there.'

Silence.

'So, what shall we do?' asks Carrot.

'Go and talk to it,' says Brian.

'But what if it's not a Gingoile, but a Tharg?' says Becky. 'There's not a huge difference between them as far as how they look.'

This is true. If I remember correctly, Thargs are taller, their second thumb is more finger-like, they have more protruding cheekbones and…

'Moustaches!' I whisper excitedly.

The others look at me as if to say "and"?

'Thargs don't have moustaches!' I continue. 'Brian, you've obviously got the best eyesight here, has that thing in the tree got a moustache?'

Brian concentrates and stares. Stares and concentrates. After about 10 seconds, which feels more like 10 minutes, he replies.

'There is definitely something on his face, a moustache is probably the nearest thing to it!'

Good. No Thargs yet, then.

'It could be a disguise,' blurts out Carrot. 'He could have put a moustache on to try and catch us out.'

'If he's wearing a disguise,' says Liz, 'why is he hiding up a tree? He could just come out and hide behind his moustache!'

Good point.

'I suppose so,' replies Carrot. 'Thought I'd mention it, just in case.'

'Ok,' I say, 'if it's just a Gingoile, shall we just walk ahead like normal?'

'I guess so,' answers Liz.

'Right, lead on Carrot.'

I wave my arm in a "troops advance meets Shakespearean bow" kind of way. (We went and saw A Midsummer Night's Dream at The New Vic in London a few months ago. It made so much sense to me that the only thing I can remember is the elaborate bowing at the end!)

'I think it's someone else's turn to take point; don't you Eddie?'

Carrot. The bravest one amongst us until we come across another living being!

'Alright Carrot,' I say. There's no point making an issue out of it, is there? 'I'll lead.'

I make my way to the front.

51

'No, it's ok Eddie. I'll lead.' It's Brian. Maybe his visionary skills have given him a new lease of confidence. 'We must protect you at all times.'

Liz and Becky exchange glances. Carrot clearly doesn't care who goes at the front as long as it's not him. In fact, he's at the back before Brian's finished saying that he'll go at the front!

'Thanks Brian,' I say. Well, it's the least I can say, even to Brian, when he puts his own life before mine.

'That's ok Eddie. After all; it's me who says it's a Gingoile, so it's me who should face it first.' And off he strides!

We all follow a bit tentatively. There's a gap opening up between Brian and the rest of us.

Then an apple, or a piece of fruit that looks like an apple, flies out of the tree straight towards Brian's head. I can see it, but I can't react quick enough to open my mouth to warn Brian. Brian calmly, but extremely swiftly, takes a side-step and avoids the flying fruit with ease.

'Is that the best you can do, Gingoile?' says Brian as he glares up in to the tree and fixes his gaze on the fruit flinger. We all stop a few yards behind Brian and wait for the response.

'Very good!' is the reply. 'And I thought you hadn't seen me.'

'We saw you,' replies Brian, 'and I could tell that you were a Gingoile and not a Tharg as well!'

On this the Gingoile drops out of the tree and lands just in front of Brian.

'Well done,' says the Gingoile. 'Besides your size, Medwick thought that you might be the weak link in the side.'

The initiative has been taken from Brian. The conversation has become too long. He turns and looks towards me for support.

'Hello,' I say. 'There are no weak links in our side. We just didn't make all our strengths clear to Medwick. If we had, we would have lost our element of surprise, wouldn't we?'

'Indeed,' says the Gingoile walking towards me and offering his hand, 'and you must be Eddie. I'm Chadwick, Medwick's cousin. Delighted to meet you at long last.'

We shake hands.

'What were you doing in the tree?' asks Becky.

'Just observing you and seeing if you were aware of your surroundings, my dear. And thanks to this one,' Chadwick points towards Brian, 'you have passed your first test with flying colours.' Brian smiles and visibly expands with pride. 'But some of the Thargs, I'm rather reluctant to say, are even cleverer than me, so don't get over-confident!'

Brian deflates slightly.

'Now, my cottage is a short distance this way.' He points down the road we intend to take towards the river. 'Come and have some lunch with me.'

Everyone smiles. Medwick and Herf did say that most of the Gingoiles that we would meet would probably feed us. Lovely!

*

They didn't taste much like apples, those things that Chadwick threw at Brian. He'd kept a few in his pockets and we had them for dessert. They were a strange flavour really. They had the texture of a pear and the flavour of a blackberry. Or was it blackcurrant? Oh, I don't know. Anyway, they looked like apples, flew through the air like apples, but they didn't taste like them!

'Are you planning to reach the village by sunset?' asks Chadwick.

'Yes,' I say, 'is that possible?'

'Oh yes. Head for Flounge's cottage, fourth on the left. He'll look after you.'

'Flounge? Ok.'

They certainly have funny names these Gingoiles. I suppose ours are equally as funny to them.

'Is he a cousin of Medwick as well?' asks Liz.

'Oh no,' replies our host, 'but I think he's a distant relative of Herf's; or at least he gives the impression of being related to Herf!'

He winks towards Liz. I don't think he's being unkind towards Herf. I think he's possibly suggesting that he might get a bit excited by our presence!

'Will we see you again?' says Becky.

'Oh, you never know, I may pop up again, or down again,' says Chadwick, patting Brian on the shoulder.

We all laugh.

'Thanks, Chadwick,' I say.

'You're welcome, young Eddie. Good Luck.'

The others say their farewells as I lead us back out into the bright sunshine.

I wonder what Chadwick meant when he said that he "may pop up again"? Surely he was joking. There's no way that he could appear ahead of us again, is there? Unless there's a short cut. But if there was a quicker route to The Dark Castle why didn't he, or Medwick or Herf, tell us about it? I don't know. Maybe I'm making something out of nothing here. It was probably just a Gingoile figure of speech. Nothing more, nothing less.

\*

This short cut idea has been going around my head. We've been walking for about two more hours and I haven't thought about much else. We've chatted occasionally, but we've agreed not to talk too much just in case someone is in earshot. Therefore, we've been thinking. I say "we" because I assume we've all been thinking. Obviously I only *know* that I've been thinking! I might have considered the possibility that maybe Brian hadn't been thinking and that his mind was just a blank, but the way he spotted Chadwick hiding up in those trees proves that there is more to everyone than meets the eye.

Whenever I've considered the possibility of there being a short cut, I'm sure that I've felt some warmth coming from my wooden box tucked inside my jacket. But whenever I've put my hand inside my jacket to feel it, it's just felt normal. Is it trying to help, again? Maybe I should mention it to the others? The thing is, we still don't know if warmth is good. Oh, I don't know. Maybe I'm thinking too much!

'There's the village,' says Brian. He's kept himself at the front since our encounter with Chadwick. Carrot is bringing up the rear.

'It's very quiet,' says Becky, 'and very quaint.'

Brian gives me another of his puzzled glances.

'Yes,' I say, 'it is very pretty.'

Brian nods. The "what does quaint mean"? is no longer on his lips.

'Lead on, Brian. Fourth cottage on the left.'

'Ok.'

He strides off, leaving us straggling behind a bit.

'Can he count to four?' says Liz.

'Come on now,' says Becky, 'be fair.'

Liz gives a wry grin. Maybe Brian is becoming more popular the further we go into The Realm.

The village is quaint. The higgledy-piggledy cottages, mostly either yellow or pink in colour, line each side of the track we're on. There are a few trees in between the cottages and, some distance away, what seems to be a well in the middle of crossroads. Maybe the well marks the centre of the village?

'Come in Brian, come in!' There is a small, plump Gingoile approaching Brian at a pace, with his arms whirling around his head in excitement.

'It looks like the owner of cottage number four has found Brian before we've had any chance of watching him count so high!' is Liz's response to the situation. Becky gives her a "look".

I'm more concerned with the fact that this Gingoile, whom I assume to be Flounge, not only knows Brian's name, but also which one of us Brian is.

'Hello Brian! Pleased to meet you!'

He grabs Brian by the hand and shakes it quite violently. Brian, to his credit, doesn't fade away from the situation, but he doesn't say anything. We've all caught up with him by now.

'Hello, are you Flounge?' I ask.

'Indeed, I am, yes, indeed I am!' He is shaking my hand as violently as he was shaking Brian's. He's definitely related to Herf. 'And you must be Eddie!'

'I am,' I say, 'but how do you know that?'

I can't help it. I have to find out straight away.

'Eddie, that's a bit rude.'

It's Liz. She's right. I was too forceful and abrupt with my enquiry. I've only just met the poor man. (Well, poor Gingoile... you know what I mean!)

'What I mean is –' I'm going to try and redeem myself now '– that our presence in The Realm is meant to be kept as quiet as possible. So how come Flounge not only knows our names, but knows which name goes with which face?'

Everyone's stare turns from me to Flounge. It looks like the rest of the gang would like an answer as well!

'Chadwick told me you were on your way,' is the excited Gingoile's reply.

'When?' asks Carrot glancing at his watch. 'We only left him a few hours ago.'

'It must have been within that time period then. Come on in, quick, before we attract any more attention.'

I had noticed the odd Gingoile face appearing at cottage numbers one to three. Flounge has turned and bustled off towards his cottage. We have no choice but to follow. I'm determined to question Flounge further on the questions he is trying to avoid.

*

These Gingoiles really know how to eat. Before any of us had any chance of asking Flounge anything at all, there we all were, being seated round another huge table covered with mounds of food.

We've all settled down now away from the table in what can only be described as bean bags without the beans in! They seem to be filled with golden syrup or black treacle! We're all wallowing around. The girls are giggling and Brian, well, I think Brian may be in his for a very long time!

'Can I use your phone, please Flounge?'

It's Carrot. What's he up to?

'What's a phone?' replies Flounge.

'You know, the thing you and Chadwick communicated with just before we arrived. I'm assuming it's like the phones we have on Earth.'

I see where Carrot is coming from now; keep going! There's a pause. Flounge is thinking very hard.

'We communicate differently in The Realm,' is Flounge's long awaited reply.

'How?' presses Carrot.

'I can't say!'

'Why not?' joins in Becky.

'Medwick told me not to!'

'So, you've been talking to Medwick *as well* as Chadwick have you Flounge?' says Liz, coming in with a tone I've only ever heard on TV!

'We all talk to each other like you do on your phones, just in a different way. I mustn't tell you how, you must work it out yourselves!'

We all look at Flounge. None of us have seen a Gingoile on the verge of losing their temper!

You know where your rooms are,' continues the grumpy Gingoile. 'I'll see you in the morning.' He's gone.

'Well,' says Liz, 'I think we might've hit a nerve there!'

'Why can't he tell us how they communicate with each other?' says Carrot.

Why indeed?

'I have an idea.' I haven't, but I don't want the troops to lose faith! 'But I think I need to sleep on it! Let's go to bed and discuss this further in the morning.'

# Chapter Seven

Yes, yes, yes. The box has done it again. I lay there, in bed, thinking about communicating without using phones and I thought of transporting; you know like in Star Trek, and as soon as I thought of that, my box began to warm up and glow. But this time it glowed in just one corner. Within the warm area were two symbols: a well and a cave. These must be transportation places and now it's light I'm going to look at the map.

'The map, Carrot, quick!'

'What?' He's not properly awake yet.

'The map! I think I'm on to something. I need the map!'

'Oh, right.' Off he goes. One pocket, another pocket, a further pocket, a fourth pocket, bingo! (I hope I never need to ask him for something in a *real* hurry!)

'What have you worked out, Eddie?'

'Hang on, Carrot!'

Now, I don't want to tell the others until I'm sure... yes! There it is, a small well marked in the middle of the village we're in.

'What is it, Eddie?' I think he can tell that I'm getting a bit excited!

'Wait just a few more seconds, Carrot.' Got it. The cave is about halfway between the village we're in and The Palace of The Realm.

'Yes!' I shout. 'Got it!'

'Well don't give it to me!' It's Brian turning over in bed. 'I need more sleep, you two were snoring all night.'

Carrot and I look at each other in disbelief. Us two snoring? Maybe we were, but there's no way that we were louder than him. No way on this Earth... well, Realm.

Carrot looks like he's about to open his mouth and probably say something to Brian about his snoring.

'Leave it, Carrot,' I say, 'just get him out of his bed and wake the girls up. I'm going to get Flounge and show you what I think I've worked out.'

58

*

'Transportation!' Looks of bewilderment from all except Flounge. 'Transportation!' The repetition of the word hasn't helped. 'Do you want to explain, Flounge, or shall I?'

'I don't know what you're talking about, Master Eddie, I really don't!' The quite apparent quiver in his voice is suggesting otherwise.

'Ok, have it your way.' I turn to the others. 'I believe that the Gingoiles communicate with each other by transporting themselves, in person, to different places within The Realm.'

'Is this true, Flounge?' asks my sis.

Flounge's eyes sink down towards the floor.

'I think it is,' I continue. 'When I thought of the idea overnight, my box glowed and became warm on these two symbols.' I show them the small carvings of the well and the cave on one of the long sides of the box. 'There's a well in the village, I saw it when we arrived, and a cave halfway between here and the Palace, therefore we cut out two or three days walking by using this short cut; by transportation.'

'Is it safe?' asks Becky.

'Well, Flounge, is it safe?' I repeat.

The Gingoile raises his head. 'Oh, please don't tell Medwick that I told you, he will be so annoyed with me.'

'But you didn't,' says Carrot, 'Eddie worked it out for himself.' Thanks mate.

'I know he did, but I feel like I gave you clues last night and, anyway, Medwick won't believe me when I say that I didn't help; I'm always getting things wrong.'

'Why did Medwick say that you couldn't help us?' I ask.

'Because you must work everything out yourself.'

'Why?' questions Carrot.

'Medwick says that the more you work out for yourself, the better prepared you will be when you get to The Dark Castle.'

'I suppose that makes sense,' I say.

'Could we have transported here?' asks Brian. 'Instead of walking?'

'Yes,' replies Flounge, 'there's a transporter quite near to Medwick's residence. The tree on the box, to the left of the well, is the sign for that one.' He points it out for us all to see.

'So, the transporter sites are in order around the box, are they, Flounge?' I ask.

'Sort of,' is his rather stuttering reply. 'I really mustn't help.'

'That's alright Flounge, and when I next see Medwick I will tell him that you didn't help us at all, ok?' I try to reassure our friend.

'Thank you, young Eddie, that would be most appreciated.'

He smiles his moustache-covered smile.

'We still don't know if it's safe!' repeats Becky.

'Oh yes,' answers a slightly rejuvenated Flounge, 'I can tell you that. It's perfectly safe. You just step on to the marked zone, it's quite apparent, and a split second later you're at the next site.'

'Can we get on one and appear right by the Castle?' It's Brian. He seems desperate to avoid walking!

'No, Brian,' answers Flounge, 'the well goes to Medwick's tree or to the cave. You can't jump any further than one site at a time. There's a set route and we can't be going too far at a time. That might not be good for us.'

'When we step on the zone, how do we know whether we're going to appear in the cave or at Medwick's tree?' Good question Carrot.

'Again,' replies Flounge, 'that's all quite apparent from the markings on the zone.'

There's a pause in the proceedings.

'I'm sorry that I wasn't much help,' starts up Flounge, again!

'That's ok, you've been a great host,' I say, 'hasn't he, everyone?'

'Yes,' says Liz, giving Flounge a big hug. That's cheered him up!

'We better go and find this well, hadn't we Eddie?'

'Yes Carrot,' I reply, 'we should be off.'

'I've topped all your knapsacks up,' says Flounge. 'There should be enough there to keep you going.'

'I'm still full up from all the food I ate yesterday!' says Brian. The girls giggle. If Big Brian is that full, you can imagine how full the rest of us are!

'Is the well down the hill, further into the village?' asks Carrot.

'Yes, not far, you won't miss it,' answers Flounge. 'It's still quite early and I doubt if many other Gingoiles are awake. I'd just head straight for it as quick as possible, if I were you.'

'Ok, thank you Flounge,' I say. 'We might see you again!'

I pick up my knapsack and head to the door while the others say their farewells and grab their bags.

*

'That was easy enough, wasn't it, Eddie?' asks Carrot.

We're standing by the well.

'Well, we're here in one piece without anyone seeing us, so I guess so!' I reply.

'Two Gingoiles saw us!' announces Brian.

'Really?' says a rather shocked Carrot. The girls start to look around.

'Yes,' replies Brian, 'one was looking out of an upstairs window two cottages down from Flounge's, and another was looking out of a downstairs window a bit further down on the other side of the road.'

My word! Eagle-eyes Brian has done it again!

'With eyesight like that,' says Becky, 'maybe we should rename Brian, Carrot!' We all laugh, except Brian.

'Why?' he asks. We all look towards Becky.

''Coz,' she continues, 'you're said to have good eyesight, particularly at night, if you eat lots of carrots.'

'Oh, right, well I suppose I do eat a lot of carrots,' is Brian's rather surprising reply.

'Really?' I say, trying not to sound too surprised. I mean, when you look at him, fruit and veg is the last thing you visualise him eating. He looks more like a meat, chocolate and sticky toffee pudding kind of person!

'I give my rabbit a carrot every day and I probably eat half of it as I'm walking down the garden to give it to him.'

'I didn't know you had a rabbit,' says Liz.

'Nor did I,' joins in Becky, 'what's his name?'

'It's M…'

'Hang on,' buts in Carrot. Our Carrot, not *a* carrot! 'Aren't we supposed to be doing this quickly?

'Eh?' says Becky.

'This zone thing; aren't we supposed to be getting on it, getting in to the cave and getting out of sight before Gingoiles three, four and five see us as well?

'You're right, Carrot,' I say. 'I'll go first, check it's ok, then come back and get the rest of you, ok?'

The girls nod.

'Sure,' says Brian.

'No,' says Carrot.

'Why not?' I ask.

''Coz we're supposed to be protecting you,' he continues. 'What if there's a Tharg hanging around in the cave, what would happen then?' What indeed!

'I suppose you're right,' I say. 'Are you going to go first, Carrot?'

Let's see if it's the brave Carrot with us today!

'Err, no.' Oh dear, it's the pizza monster fearing Carrot! 'I thought that Brian should go first,' he continues, 'seeing as his eyesight is so good and it might be dark at the other end. What with it being a cave.'

That's logical, I guess.

'Well, Brian, it's up to you, do you want to go first?' I ask, fully expecting no more than a shrug of his shoulders.

'Ok, but what do I do?'

Blimey, a decisive answer, just when we need one!

'Well,' I say, 'I guess you stand on this half of the zone.'

I point towards the zone, which we've all been standing around for the last few minutes. It's oval in shape, with a drawing of a tree on one half of the oval and a drawing of the mouth of a cave on the other. There's only really room for one person on each half, maybe two, at a push.

'And what do I do at the other end to come back?' asks the confused and ever so slightly worried looking Brian.

'I guess,' and this time I really am guessing! 'that you step off of the zone and then step back on to the picture of the well.'

'What would a picture of a well look like?'

Carrot's head drops. The girls don't giggle. A day or two earlier they would have, but we're all recognising that Brian, like all of us, has his own strengths and weaknesses. Giggling at his weaknesses will only make him less confident in using his strengths, such as his size and his excellent eyesight.

'It will probably look something like this.'

I turn and point to the well a couple of feet behind me.

'Oh right,' replies Brian with a slightly sheepish grin.

'Off you go, then.' I try and say in my most encouraging voice. 'When you get to the other end, look around, check that the coast is clear, step off the zone and then back on to it, ok?'

'I think so Eddie, I'll do my best,' answers a now sweating Brian.

'If you're not back in a couple of minutes one of us will come after you, won't we, Eddie?' says Becky.

'Oh yes, of course,' I say, 'but it won't come to that.' I hope!

'Ok,' says Brian, 'see you in a minute.'

And with that, he steps onto the zone. One, two, he's gone! He just vanished.

'Wow!' says Liz.

'Time him, Carrot,' I ask. 'Give him two minutes from now.'

We wait. In silence. The disappearing was amazing. No shimmering or funny noises, like in Star Trek. He just went!

'I wish he'd hurry up,' says Becky, 'I'm sure there's a Gingoile watching us from that window over there.'

She nods towards a cottage. I think she's right.

'Don't worry about that,' says Liz, 'worry about Brian.'

'How long has it been, Carrot?' I enquire.

'Forty-four seconds,' he replies without taking his eyes off of his watch.

'Is that all?' asks Liz.

'Forty-eight, now!' is Carrot's rather deadpan reply.

'What's forty-eight?' It's Brian. He's reappeared just like that. No noise, just reappearance!

'What happened,' asks Becky, 'did it hurt?'

'Did you see anything at the other end?' asks Carrot.

'Hang on,' says Liz, raising her voice over those of Becky and Carrot, 'give him a chance to speak!'

'Ok,' I say, 'quickly and calmly, Brian, tell us what happened.'

Brian takes a deep breath.

'I stepped on that,' he points towards the zone, 'and one second I was looking at you lot and then I was looking at nothing!'

'What do you mean,' I ask, 'did you end up in a cave?'

'Well, it was pitch black and cold, so I guess so.'

'Then what did you do?' I continue to press for more information.

'Well, nothing.' Nothing? 'I mean it was so dark that it doesn't matter how many carrots I've eaten; I couldn't see a thing!' We all smile at Brian's carrot reference. 'So,' he continues, 'I sort of guessed where the edge of the zone was, 'coz I couldn't even see my feet, stepped off it and then back on, and here I am!'

'Well done, Brian,' I say, patting him on his back. 'What do you make of that, Carrot?'

'Well, first of all, I think we'll need this.' He produces a small torch from one his many pockets. 'And I guess that if it was so dark that even Brian couldn't see, then even if something unpleasant was there, they wouldn't be able to see us either!' True.

'Until we turn the torch on!' says Liz. Also true.

'Do you think anyone was there, Brian?' I ask.

'No,' he replies, 'I could only smell damp, I couldn't smell any Gingoiles.'

'What do you mean, smell any Gingoiles?' asks Becky.

I was about to ask the same question!

'Well, they have their own kind of smell, don't they,' continues Brian, 'haven't you noticed it?'

'No' we all say, virtually together.

'Oh yes,' says Brian, 'all the Gingoiles we've met have very similar smells!'

Good grief! Big Brian is the King of the Senses. First his eyesight and now his sense of smell!

'But you don't know what Thargs smell like, do you Brian?' says Carrot. 'One of them could have been standing right next to you!'

Get out of that one, Sense King!

'There was only a Tharg there if Thargs smell like damp!'

What a reply! The girls giggle and even the questioning Carrot joins me in a slight chuckle.

'So,' I say, 'as long as Thargs don't smell like damp –' the girls giggle again '– there's no one there. Is that right Brian?'

'That's right, Eddie!'

Well, that's good enough for me.

'Ok,' I say, 'give Brian the torch, Carrot, unless you want to go first?'

'Err, its ok, Eddie, Brian can go first,' replies Carrot as he hands Brian the torch. I thought he'd say that!

'Off you go, Brian, I'll be right behind you. Turn the torch on now and remember to step off the zone once you're there so I don't land on your head!'

'Ok,' says Brian as he turns on the torch and steps on the zone once more. One, two and he's gone again.

'Right,' I say, 'I'll give him a couple of seconds before I go; make sure you do the same for me.'

I step onto the zone and one, two and it's dark. It's as if I didn't get transported, but everything around me has. It's as if I stood still and the village and the well and the daylight were swapped for this dark, damp, cold cave!

Hang on. Now I'm starting to focus in the dark. A couple of feet to my right stands Brian. Even though I can't see him I know it's him because there's torchlight coming from that direction. My eyes follow the beam and… oh no…

**65**

'Is that you, Eddie?' It's the voice of quite a nervous sounding Brian.

'Err, yes, Brian, it's me.' I reply, trying not to let too much of a quiver enter my voice.

'Damp, Eddie… they smell of damp!' answers Brian.

There, no more than 15 feet away, are two Thargs staring back at Brian and me.

'What's that?' It's Becky who has appeared right next to me on the zone.

'Thargs!' I splutter in response. 'Quick Becky, get back on the zone, go back to the well and keep Liz and Carrot there. Make sure you all move away from the zone.' I push Becky back onto the zone before she has a chance to reply.

'Eddie?' It's Brian. 'They're walking towards us, Eddie!' I look up. The two Thargs, looking like two heavily built, clean shaven Gingoiles, are striding towards us. 'What are we going to do Eddie?'

'We're going to see if this zone will take two at a time.' I jump on to the zone and drag Brian with me. The Thargs are getting close… one, they're about six feet away now… two, and the darkness returns to bright light as both of us return to the well.

'Oh my God, Eddie,' shouts Liz, 'are you alright?'

'Yes, but we need to act quickly. There are two Thargs in that cave and I'm banking on them following us.

'Let's run back to Flounge's house and hide!' says Carrot.

'We can't run every time we see a Tharg, can we Eddie?' adds Becky.

'No, we can't, Becky,' I reply, 'if we did that we'd never get out of the village! What we've got to do is stand here,' I position myself facing the zone with the well behind it, 'and when the Thargs appear we've got to push them into the well, ok?'

The others look at me in disbelief.

'You mean kill them, Eddie?' asks Liz.

'No, I mean push them in the well!' I say, knowing full well that the fall might kill them, or it may only give them a headache and a bath!

'It's them or us!' says Brian.

'Brian's right. Now we've got to be quick, they could be here any sec....' I'm cut short as a Tharg, bigger than me, but not as big as Brian, appears two feet in front of me.

'Help me Brian,' I shout as I lunge at the Tharg. Brian is a split second behind me and we take our enemy completely by surprise. The back of the Tharg's knees jolt against the top of the small brick wall surrounding the well. His centre of mass shifts backwards and gravity takes hold – don't you just love science!? He's gone. There's a pause and a distant splash. It's a deep well!

'Well, that wasn't too difficult was it?' I say as I'm looking down the well. Brian taps me on the shoulder. I turn around and there, standing on the zone is the second Tharg, bigger than the first, staring back. Whoops! We're the wrong side of him, now what? Suddenly there's a huge scream as Liz, Becky and Carrot hurl themselves at the back of the massive Tharg. He starts to stumble towards me and at the last second I side-step him so that he falls to join his friend.

We all stare down the well. There is a distant sound of raised voices and splashing. I think they have both survived the fall!

'Well done everyone,' I say more in relief than victory.

'Great side-step, Eddie,' says Carrot, 'just like Jason Robinson!'

Carrot is referring to a time we played rugby last winter in PE at school. Four times I had the ball with only one player to beat and each time I tried to side-step I got tackled. Our rugby fanatic of a PE teacher, Mr Greaves, said I side-stepped like Jason Robinson driving a tractor. The name only stuck with Mr Greaves until the cricket season started. He then found another one for me!

'Right, back to the cave,' I announce. 'Brian, me and the torch first, then the two girls and then you, Carrot, ok?'

'Ok!' answers Carrot more positively now we've disposed of our first Thargs.

'Just give us thirty seconds before you follow us,' I say to Liz and Becky, 'that way we have time to return again if there are any more problems.'

'Ok,' reply Becky and my sister.

'Right, Brian, torch on?'

'Torch on, Eddie!'
'Ok, let's try again!'

## Chapter Eight

Yes. No more Thargs in that cave. It wasn't too difficult getting out of the cave, not with Carrot's torch, anyway! But where now?

'Ok, Bro, where to next?'

That's just what I was thinking!

'Well,' I say as I get the box out from my pocket, 'if we're going by the symbols on the box it goes; tree, well, cave and a sort of house thing, which I hope is The Palace of the Realm. What do you think Sis?'

I pass her the box.

'I think you're right,' she says, 'but the problem is that the well had two symbols on it, didn't it? Half was showing the tree at Medwick's house and half the cave. But the symbol in the cave appeared to be only one way, there was only one big well marked on the zone. Where's the zone with The Palace of the Realm marked on it?'

I don't know! And no one else is saying much either!

'We did check all the cave with the torch, didn't we Brian?' I say.

'Yep!' is his brief reply.

'It wasn't really the world's biggest cave, was it, Eddie?' offers Carrot. 'It's not as if one of those great big zones could have been hiding in there, is it?'

'Not in that cave, no,' joins in Becky.

'What do you mean?' I reply.

'The zone might not have been hiding in that cave, but it might be in another!'

'Yes,' I say, a bit over excitedly, 'more than one cave! We walk away from this one and into another to find the part of the zone with The Palace of the Realm on it!'

'Eddie!' says Liz. Not now Sis, I'm on a flow.

'Great thinking, Becky, you see, that's why....'

'Eddie!!'

I'm still flowing Liz, can't you tell? 'That's why you're in my team, lateral thinking...'

'Eddie!!!' Liz shouts so loud I have to stop and listen.

'What is it, Liz?'

'The box; as soon as you said more than one cave it started to glow and feel warm on the cave sign! Look!' she passes the box to me. It is still slightly warm and I can see a fading glow coming from the cave symbol.

'Excellent! You were definitely right, Becky, well done!'

'Which way, then?' offers Carrot.

We all look around. We're only just outside of the cave. There's an open area in front of us. The odd tree and bush in the opening, but round the edge of this area are lots of trees and bushes, spreading into the distance and turning into woods and eventually forests.

'I can't see any caves,' says Liz, rather unenthusiastically. 'Anyone else see anything other than trees, grass, bushes and more trees?' She smiles.

I can't see anything else, but, hang on....

'Brian,' I turn to face the King of Senses, 'can you see anything?'

'Afraid not,' he says whilst still trying to pierce through the surrounding shrubs with his eyes. 'If there are any caves around here, they are hidden by the trees.'

'Ok,' says Becky, 'let's go look!' She makes to stride off into the opening.

'Hang on,' joins in Carrot, 'is it safe to just go walking off like that?'

He's right, you know.

'He's right, you know' I say. 'I think we should stick together and gradually work our way through the trees until we find the cave, ok?'

'Ok,' says Carrot, who is clearly in pizza monster fearing mode at present. The others just look around.

'Have you seen how big this area is Eddie?' It's my sis, really sounding like a sis! 'And how many trees there are?'

I know,' I reply, 'but the cave can't be too far away. If it was, there would be a separate symbol on my box, wouldn't there?'

'Maybe,' says Liz, 'but I still think we should spread out. I don't like the look of those clouds. I think the weather may be taking a turn

70

for the worse. The sooner we find it, the sooner we can be safe in the Palace.'

'I suppose you're right.' I'm not sure she is, but she has a good point with regards to the weather. 'We'll spread out then, ok?'

'Ok,' say Brian and Becky.

Carrot nods in a "not too impressed" way.

'Right,' I announce, 'spread out, don't go out into the open area, stay in the trees and bushes and meet back here in fifteen minutes, ok?'

'Ok' is the almost uniform reply as they all check their watches.

Off we go!

\*

Now I'm on my own I get a very strong feeling that I shouldn't have been swayed so easily by Liz. I kept an eye on the others for as long as I could, particularly Carrot who was walking like his hair; gingerly! I've now been searching for five minutes. Trees, bushes, the odd boulder, but nothing more. I hope one of the others finds it. These trees are becoming much denser than I had anticipated. Liz might be right about the clouds making it darker, but in here it doesn't make much difference. What light there is, is struggling to penetrate the entwining treetops. Well, that's it. Seven and a half minutes this way. I better make my way back. I hope Brian has thought about how far to go, time-wise, before turning back!

\*

'I've found it!' shouts Becky who's already at the meeting point.

'Ssh!' I say as I get nearer to her. 'Remember to be careful!'

'Sorry,' she says more quietly. 'I've found it; just a few minutes that way,' she points. 'I walked into this really dense bush and found

71

an opening to a cave. The zone was just inside. I've been back here ages!'

'Fantastic!' I say. 'We'll go as soon as the others arrive.'

'I'm sorry I'm late!' It's Brian, jogging towards us.

'Why are you running? Is someone chasing you?' I say, trying to stay calm.

'No,' puffs Brian, 'no one's chasing me; it's just that after searching for ten minutes I realised that it would take me ten minutes to get back again, so I ran!'

I knew it! Well at least he worked it out after ten minutes and not the whole fifteen!

'It doesn't matter, Brian,' I say in a "well done" kind of manner. 'You're only a minute late; I just hope you didn't draw any attention to yourself by running through the woods.'

'I did try and do it as quietly as I could, Eddie.'

'It doesn't look like anyone's followed you, Brian,' says Becky. She gives him a warm smile. Brian's tongue flicks out to prevent any drooling.

'What about the other two?' I say, glancing at my watch. 'They're almost three minutes late!'

'Maybe they've done the same as me, Eddie?' offers Brian.

'I don't want to be rude, Brian, but I don't think that either my sister or Carrot would make that mistake. What do you think, Becky?'

'I don't think they would either, Eddie, but what I do think is that it's starting to rain!'

She's right. Warm, seemingly warmer than at home, and wet rain is starting to fall.

'What should we do, Eddie?' asks Becky.

'I don't know,' is my rather useless reply. 'Did either of you hear anything that might have suggested that someone's kidnapped them?'

'Oh, surely not, Eddie. Nobody's kidnapped them,' says Becky. 'They've either got lost or they're running late.'

'Or their watches have stopped!' joins in Brian.

I ignore that last remark.

'So, neither of you heard anything then?' I continue.

'No,' replies Becky.

'No,' follows Brian, 'or maybe I did!'

'What do you mean, "maybe you did", Brian?' I say rather abruptly.

'Well, I'd just stopped to turn round and come back again when I heard a faint rustling in the distance. I thought it was just an animal or a bird, but it might have been something else.'

'From which direction was the noise coming?' I probe.

'That way.' Brian points.

'That's towards the cave that I found!' jumps in Becky.

'I could be wrong,' I say, 'but I think that both Liz and Carrot have been caught by Thargs.' A shiver goes down my spine as I speak. 'They could have been taken through the forest or to either of the caves with zones in. And seeing as Brian says he heard the noise near the new zone, I'm guessing they've been taken towards The Palace of the Realm.'

'Why would they go there, Eddie?' asks Becky. 'There are Gingoiles all around the Palace.'

'I'm guessing that they're heading back to The Dark Castle with them; it is the quickest way.' There's a pause as the severity of our situation begins to sink in. I can't believe I let the group split up. Becky and Brian have bowed their heads. I need to lift their spirits and find my sister and my best friend.

'Right,' I continue, 'well done our King of Senses!' I pat Brian on his back. 'Let's go and find this cave. Lead on Becky!'

\*

'It's in there?' I ask, pointing at the world's most dense bush.

'Yes!' is Becky's reply. 'Just through the bush and in the opening of a small cave.'

'What on earth made you look in there?' I pry.

'I don't know,' says Becky.

'Maybe you've got a sixth sense!' says Brian.

A smile, or more of a beam, comes across Brian's face. Becky smiles back. There isn't time for all this smiling!

'Do you want to go first?' I ask Becky. 'Seeing as you found it.'

'I don't mind,' she replies. 'I will if you want me to.'

'I'd rather go first,' chips in Brian.

'Why?' I say, although I think I already know why.

''Coz it might not be safe for Becky,' he continues. 'The Thargs that got the others might be waiting at the other end of this zone.' He beams his oversized beam at Becky once more. She begins to blush slightly. Good grief. Brian; her hero!

'Ok, Brian, you go first. If you're not back in thirty seconds Becky will follow, then me. Remember to step off the zone once at the other end, and if there are Thargs at the other end come back straight away, ok?'

'Ok, Eddie,' is Brian's swift reply.

'Good luck, Brian,' adds Becky.

With a smile on his drooling lips Brian disappears into the bush.

'I hope he's ok,' says Becky.

'He'll be fine,' I say as I look at my watch. 'Ok, there's thirty seconds, off you go.'

'Ok, Eddie, see you soon,' she says as she pushes herself into the bush.

Just me now. I suppose I should have gone second really, so as to avoid being left on my own. Another mistake. What am I doing? Ok; thirty seconds.

The bush is dense but, thankfully, not prickly. Yep. The zone is marked with a palace. Please let there be no Thargs, please! Here I go....

*

'Hello Eddie!'

I look up from the zone as I step off of it.

'Hello Eddie!'

I look around. It's very bright and my eyes are finding it difficult to adjust from the dark of the caves and the wood. Nearly there. I know those voices. Oh no. I realise, with a sinking feeling, that it's Medwick and Herf.

'Hello Medwick. Hello Herf,' I say in a rather sheepish fashion whilst squinting in their general direction.

Medwick and Herf are standing with six other Gingoiles and Liz, Carrot, Becky and Brian. They are all staring at me.

'Thank God you're alright Liz.' I give her a hug. 'And you, Carrot!' I smile at him as I let go of Liz. He returns a slight smile.

'They are lucky,' booms Medwick.

'Very lucky!' adds Herf.

'You separated!' continues Medwick. 'Why did you separate when Herf told you that you needed to be a group of five, six or seven to achieve anything?'

I really want to say that it was Liz's fault, I mean it was her who suggested it, but I know that I'm supposed to be the leader and I should not have been swayed.

'I'm sorry,' I say to Medwick. 'I made a bad decision.'

'You made two!' blurts out the ever-helpful Herf.

'I know,' I say very quickly before Medwick can add any more, 'I let both Brian and Becky transport before me, rather than one each side of me.'

'Two mistakes, young Eddie,' continues Medwick. 'Liz and Carrot could have been taken by Thargs whilst wandering around on their own, and you could have been taken whilst you were on your own in the cave in the wood.'

What do I say? My four friends are staring at me. Eight Gingoiles, including six who haven't even been introduced to me, are staring at me. What do I say?

I know what to say.

'We are at The Palace of the Realm, aren't we?'

'Yes,' replies Medwick.

'Good!' I say. 'Thanks for telling us about the transporters, Medwick!'

There, take that. I'm heir to the throne, a bit of help would be nice!

'Whoops!' mutters Herf.

'That'll do, Herf,' reprimands Medwick. 'Eddie, you may think that I should have told you about the transporters; but you need to listen very carefully to me. You need to *learn* about The Realm before you can save it. If I tell you everything I know that you need to know you may think you know it, but you won't *feel* it. You need to *love* The Realm like your Uncle Mark and like us Gingoiles do. I advised you as much as I could before you set off, but things in life mean so much more to you if you have discovered them and worked them out for yourself.'

Medwick pauses. I think I understood that. Well, most of it. The bit about knowing what I need to know but not really knowing it but just thinking that I know it was just a tad confusing.

'You're good at maths at school, aren't you Eddie?'

'Yes,' I say as Medwick continues his lecture.

'Because you know whether you're right or wrong?'

'I guess so.'

'But what about art and music? You don't think you're very good at them, do you?'

'No, I don't,' is my reply.

I'm not sure where he's going with this. Carrot, Liz and Becky look bemused. Brian looks dumbfounded.

'Why don't you think you're any good at those subjects?' continues the lecturer.

''Coz my teachers tell me I'm not very good!'

'Fair enough, but do you enjoy doing those subjects?'

I think for a bit, just a little bit though.

'Yes, I do!' I reply.

'Why?' he presses.

'Because I can do what I want. Because there is no right or wrong, well not like in maths, and I can use my own free will and discover things and ways of improving myself and my work as I go along.'

Blimey. Did I really just say all that?

'Exactly, young Eddie!' says Medwick, raising a smile underneath his moustache.

'So,' I say, 'whether you teach me and whether I get it right or wrong isn't as important as trial and error, working things out for myself and growing to love The Realm through my own endeavour!'

Suddenly eight Gingoiles are smiling their moustache-covered smiles at me. Four humans are still looking bemused!

'You discovered the transporters through your own endeavour,' says Medwick.

'You defeated two Thargs through your own endeavour,' adds Herf excitedly, 'and spotted Chadwick in the tree!'

'That wasn't just me. Brian spotted Chadwick and we all got the Thargs down the well.'

'Exactly, Eddie,' says Medwick, 'you're a team, each with your own specialities. That's why you've got to stick together.'

'I know,' I say quite sheepishly.

'I know you know,' adds Medwick. Oh no, not the "I know what you know" bit again! 'You realised both of your mistakes almost before they happened. Now you need to make sure you do spot them before they happen.'

Silence.

I don't know what the others are thinking, but all I'm thinking is that was all a bit heavy! I think I understood. Well, most of it!

'Eddie?' It's Liz. 'Are you ok?'

'Yeah. Just a bit tired, that's all.'

'And hungry?' bursts out Herf. 'I hope you're all hungry. We've laid on such a feast in the Palace to welcome you. There's small pastry finiettes, bowls and bowls of graw leaves; lovely. Several bottles of my very own papberry wine; '63. Flounge has brought some...'

Medwick is waving his hands in front of Herf's face. He's been doing it for about ten seconds now. Herf stops talking.

'Thank you Herf,' says Medwick sharply, 'there's plenty of time for that when the banquet begins. First of all, I think Eddie and his friends need to be taken to their rooms to relax and freshen up. Would you like that?'

'Oh, yes,' says Becky. 'A bath. Do you think I could have a bath?'

'Yeah, and me,' says Brian rather surprisingly, 'can I have a bath too?' Brian throws his smile at an embarrassed Becky once more. Now I see why he wants a bath!

'Of course you can,' says Medwick, 'there are more than enough baths for one each in the Palace.'

'Oh, don't bother running one 'specially for me, I'm more than happy to share one with...'

'Brian!!' blasts Liz. She beat me to it. I was starting on the B when she was saying the N! 'A bath *each* would be lovely Medwick, thank you,' finishes off my sis whilst aiming her death glare at Brian.

Brian is now looking at his feet.

'Cherxil, could you go ahead and get five baths sorted out for our guests?' asks Medwick.

'Certainly, Medwick,' answers one of the six unintroduced Gingoiles.

'Is it safe to have a banquet?' I ask Medwick. 'Won't the Thargs be suspicious?'

'It won't be quite as grand as Herf may have suggested, but we should be ok. There haven't been any sitings of Thargs around here for quite some time.'

'What about the Thargs at the well?' asks Carrot.

'They came past here weeks ago,' replies Medwick, 'they must have been hanging around in the woods and caves until you attracted them to the well.'

'Haven't they alerted any other Thargs yet?' asks Liz.

'Oh no. Don't you worry about them. They are still down the well. The villagers are feeding them and keeping them quiet!'

Interesting.

'Cherxil should have those baths running by now, let's go.'

*

This bath is wonderful. I always shower at home. I can't remember the last time I had a bath. Yes, I can. A couple of years ago Liz and I stayed with our grandparents for a week. We usually stay for just a weekend and I get away with using the basin for a wash, but faced with a week I had to give in and have a bath. They don't have a shower. I don't recall enjoying that bath as much as this one. Their bath is white with little cracks all over it. It always has a grubby bath mat in it and rusty grab handles on the sides. The ancient water heater thing is on the wall above one end of the bath and every time you turn the hot tap on there's a huge whooshing noise and flames lick out of the hole you look in to see if the pilot light is lit. I remember spending about three minutes in the bath and then sitting on the edge and making splashing noises with my hand just in case someone was listening at the door making sure I was in there!

This is nothing like that. This bath is fantastic. The bath is long and wide. It's pure white, no cracks in it, the taps are on the side and they look like gold! I don't know if they're real gold, I don't know how to tell. I bet Carrot knows how to tell. He's probably doing some test on one of his taps right now.

The whole Palace is amazing. All pure, bright white. We haven't seen much yet. Just the front, which is vast with lots of columns and windows; the massive entrance hall with three beautiful chandeliers, and then up the grand staircase to our rooms. Carrot, Brian and I are sharing a bedroom. Medwick told us we could have one each, but after what happened today, I thought it was better if we shared a room! Liz and Becky are sharing a room a couple of doors down a corridor from us.

But we all have our own bath!

*

'Unbelievable!' says Carrot. The rest of us just stare around the banquet hall with our mouths wide open. It is extraordinary. Huge; with columns, paintings, carvings and sculptures. Wonderful!

'The Thargs could live here, but they choose to live in The Dark Castle!' says Becky.

'And they don't choose The Dark Castle because it's better,' says Herf, 'oh no, it's because it's dark and dirty and miserable like the Thargs themselves. When Zendorf and some of his cronies stayed here they left because they were worried that all the brightness, cleanliness and joy that fills the Palace might rub off on them. And they couldn't have that, could they?'

'Thank you, Herf,' says Medwick in his usual manner when faced with Herf and his gossip, 'go and help Denflet open those bottles of papberry you brought.'

'Ok,' says Herf as he scurries away.

'Now, friends,' continues Medwick, 'do you all feel refreshed and ready for some food?'

'Oh yes!' says Brian as if he's starving. We all laugh.

'Young Brian, yes, you must be hungry,' says Medwick, 'you are a growing lad, after all!' We continue to laugh.

'All I must say is try a bit of every food. Some may remind you of food from home, some may be a completely new taste sensation. Just go carefully with Herf's papberry wine. It's good, and the '63 is a particularly good year, but intersperse it with some Hanjarl punch. It has a certain alkalinity that punches the acidity of the pap, so that you remain on your feet!'

Everyone smiles at me.

'In other words,' I quickly add, 'don't get drunk! We've got a lot more walking to do tomorrow.'

'Ok, Eddie,' say Brian, Carrot and Becky as they head off towards the food and the twenty or so Gingoiles who are joining us for the banquet.

'Just you be careful yourself, Bro,' adds Liz as she ruffles my hair and goes off to join the others.

I don't know. I'm heir to a throne and my sister still insists on ruffling my hair! Does she do it just because she's my sister, or because she's taller than me? She must know I'll overtake her in height one day and I'll ruffle her back!

'Are you going to join your friends, young Eddie? There are lots of Gingoiles I want to introduce you to,' says Medwick.

'In a minute, Medwick,' I say, 'I just want to discuss the next two symbols on my box.'

'Relax, young Eddie. We can do that in the morning. For now, I want you to enjoy the banquet and put all other thoughts to the back of your mind. How does that sound?'

'I might relax better if I could get a couple of questions off my chest,' I press.

'Ok, young Eddie, if it will help you relax. But don't take too long over it, Brian's already eaten half of Denflet's homemade tasana flans and they are one of my particular favourites!'

'Ok, I'll be quick,' I say as I get the box out of my pocket. 'This symbol here, next to the one of the Palace, is it a waterfall or a...' I can't finish. A hissing noise has interrupted me. A cloud of smoke is welling up at the far end of the room. Everyone is moving swiftly towards the end of the room where Medwick and I are standing.

'What's going on, Medwick?' asks Liz as she's walking towards us.

'I don't know,' is Medwick's reply. He follows this with a wave of the hand and six Gingoiles leave the room by various exits. I think they are the same Gingoiles we met by the zone. They must be security.

'Should we leave the hall, Medwick?' I ask. 'It could be a poisonous gas.'

'No, young Eddie. I believe it is just smoke and it appears to be beginning to disappear!'

He's right. The smoke cloud is disappearing. Something is now behind it. A person? A Gingoile? A.......... I don't know. It's big. It's huge.......... No moustache. A Tharg?

'Zendorf!' exclaims Medwick in a controlled whisper.

'Zendorf?' I reply as my friends stare in disbelief, or is it horror.

'Yes,' repeats Medwick, 'Zendorf.'

# Chapter Nine

'You thought I was in The Dark Castle didn't you, you despicable Gingoiles! Well, I'm here amongst you, in my Palace.'

This Zendorf does not appear to be a pleasant chap!

'Did you like my entrance?' continues Zendorf.

Who's he looking at? Zendorf seems to be looking straight across the room. I would have thought he would have been looking at me, or at least at Medwick.

'I can appear wherever and whenever I like,' continues the slightly visually challenged Zendorf. 'You will never be completely alone again!'

That's it. I've had enough of his rudeness and inability to look any of us in the eye.

'Where is he looking?' I mutter at Medwick.

'I'm not sure, young Eddie,' replies Medwick. 'I try and avoid talking to Zendorf; but when I have, he has always stared me in the eye. He thinks it's menacing. It doesn't work on me though. I find his breath more menacing than his eyes!'

Carrot and the others have moved a little closer to listen in on our conversation.

'Look, Eddie,' says Liz, 'he's not even bothered by us talking whilst he is!'

She's right. He's just continuing to drone on about his omnipresence and stuff.

'He's not here!' says Carrot.

'You what?' I say.

'He's not here!' I thought that's what he said. 'If you look at him from where I'm standing you can see the corner of the picture on the wall that's behind him straight through him. I think he's a hologram.'

I move over to look. Zendorf is still dribbling on endlessly about his power etc.

'You're right, Carrot. Plus,' I continue, 'how tall is Zendorf, Medwick? I'm sure you said that most are no taller than Brian, who is six foot.'

'You're right, young Eddie. Most are shorter than Brian. Zendorf is one of the tallest. He's around six foot three, I would say.'

'Exactly!' I exclaim. 'That Zendorf,' I say as I point, 'is at least six foot ten. That's why he appears to be looking over all of our heads rather than into our eyes!'

'Brilliant, young Eddie,' cries Medwick.

'If it's a hologram there should be some sort of transmitter. Is that right, Carrot?' I ask.

'Yes, and it will be easier to find whilst he's talking,' replies Carrot. 'When he stops talking and the image is turned off it will be virtually impossible to find.'

'And so, small Gingoiles,' continues the *hologram* of Zendorf, 'it is time for me to disappear the same way that I arrived....'

'Quick,' I say loudly to everyone in the room, 'it's not really Zendorf, it's a hologram. We have to find the transmitter quickly. Spread out!'

Carrot and I lead the way. Everyone else cottons on and joins in.

'Remember who rules The Realm,' continues the ever-annoying image of Zendorf. 'I may appear again soon....'

'Quickly everyone,' shouts Medwick, 'find the transmitter before he goes!'

'The smoke's returning!' cries Becky.

'That must be his *leaving* smoke,' I say.

'Got it!' goes up a cry from a Gingoile. The image of Zendorf is now wobbling as the Gingoile is picking up the transmitter from the base of a pot plant.

'Well done, Denflet!' says Medwick. 'Bring it to me.'

The image has gone. So has the smoke. An air of calm starts to descend on the room.

'Thank you, Denflet,' says Medwick as the transmitter is passed to him.

'Do you want this, Eddie?' says Brian as he passes another device to me.

'What's this?' I ask.

'It's the thing the smoke was coming out of,' replies Brian.

'How did you find this?'

'As the smoke was dying away, I managed to see it. It was hidden in the corner of that picture,' says Brian pointing at the picture that Carrot and I could see through the hologram of Zendorf.

My King of Senses has struck again.

'Fantastic Brian,' I say. 'Well done!'

'Yes, well done Brian,' adds Medwick.

Medwick looks at the device he is holding. I look at the one I am holding. I don't know what I am looking for. I don't really know what I'm looking at. It's small, round and quite light with a tiny hole in it where I assume the smoke came out of. The transmitter that Medwick is holding is similar, just a little bit larger. Medwick is looking much closer at his. He seems to know what he is looking at.

'It's not of The Realm,' announces Medwick after a couple of minutes of studying. 'I have no idea where this technology comes from.'

'Uncle Mark,' exclaims Liz. 'He made it!'

'What makes you say that, Sis?'

'Well, he used to work in computers; Medwick says that the technology is not of The Realm, Uncle Mark isn't of The Realm, and the Thargs have Uncle Mark prisoner. They have forced him to make the transmitters to scare the Gingoiles.'

Wow, Liz. What a fantastic deduction.

'It all makes sense, young Eddie,' says Medwick.

'Except for one thing,' says Carrot.

'What's that?' asks Liz.

'The fact that the image of Zendorf was too tall. Why make such a precise transmitter and then get the image size wrong?' adds Carrot.

'Maybe Zendorf wanted to be made bigger so that he appeared scarier to the Gingoiles,' suggests Becky.

'Maybe,' replies Carrot, 'but he was talking as if he expected us to believe he was in the room. It's scarier for the Gingoiles to believe that Zendorf can turn up anywhere without notice, rather than them to know it's just an oversized hologram. He's given the game away just by getting your Uncle Mark to make him look bigger.'

'Maybe,' I say, 'it wasn't Zendorf that gave the game away!'

They all look at me. I get nervous very quickly when they all stare expectantly. It makes me suddenly rethink what I was about to say, just in case it's gonna sound stupid.

'Maybe it was Uncle Mark.' They continue to stare. My four friends, Medwick, Herf and several other Gingoiles all glaring in my direction. All staring into my eyes. I wish they would stare over my head like the Zendorf hologram did! 'He probably convinced Zendorf that it would make him look scarier, or he just didn't mention it at all knowing that he wouldn't notice it. But he knew the change would be noticed by the Gingoiles.'

'Well, young Eddie,' says Medwick, all the eyes now shifting towards him, 'it makes sense.'

'And,' I add, I'm on one of my rolls now, 'if he's banking on us spotting the deliberate mistake then he might be banking on us finding the transmitters and he might have hidden some sort of communication or message inside one of the transmitters!' Did I really say that? Sounds a bit far-fetched really, doesn't it?

'Sounds a bit far-fetched to me, Bro.'

You'd never guess we were related, would you?

'I agree,' adds Medwick. Oh, thanks. 'But there is no harm in checking.'

Really! Wow!

'Go and fetch Professor Krunk, Herf,' continues Medwick. 'He's the only Gingoile who may have enough knowledge to access these transmitters and see if Eddie is on to something.'

'Straight away, Medwick,' says Herf. He is out of sight before his words fade away.

'Right,' says Medwick, 'that's enough interruptions from Zendorf and those dreaded Thargs. On with the banquet!'

'Great,' says Brian, 'now where were those flans?'

'Over there,' says Medwick pointing towards the drinks table. Brian wanders off excitedly.

'They're not over there,' says Becky, 'they are that way!' She waves in the opposite direction to that which Brian is heading in.

'Oh, I know,' says Medwick with a glint in his eye, 'it's just that the tasana flans are my favourite and Brian has already had so many of them. I must go and have some before he realises that I sent him the wrong way!'

He rushes off as we all look after him rather bemused!

*

And I thought the bath was good! The bed was fantastic! At least seven feet wide and eight feet long. A mattress four feet thick. Duvet filled with pure white down from the Ayck, a swan-like creature with even a longer neck according to Herf. And we had one of these each! Brian said it's the first bed he's ever slept in where his feet didn't touch the end. Mind you, he is still in one of those cabin beds at home made for the under eights! I dreamed of all strange things last night. The Realm. The journey we've been on. The journey yet to come. Brian says he dreamed of tasana flan and papberry wine; there's a surprise. Carrot says he dreamed of nothing. But he did wake me up in the night shouting "No, Zendorf, no"! I won't mention it.

'Good morning, Eddie,' says Herf, peering round the door, 'are you well?'

'Yes,' I reply, 'and you?'

'Oh, yes indeed,' answers an excited Herf, 'very well! Where are Carrot and Brian?'

'In their bathrooms.'

'Well,' continues Herf in an increasingly excited manner, 'get them to hurry up. Medwick wants to see you all as soon as possible in the hall. He has some very exciting news for you!'

He scurries off before I can reply. Exciting news, eh? I wonder what it can be.

*

'Morning, Bro.'

'Hi Sis; Becky.'

'Hello Eddie.'

'Been waiting for us long?' I say.

'Not long,' says Liz. 'Sleep ok?'

'Fine, thanks'

'Did you sleep well, Becky?' asks Brian.

'Yes, thank you...'

'Morning all!' It's Medwick entering very quickly with another Gingoile close behind. 'This is Professor Krunk,' announces Medwick.

'Good morning, everyone,' he says quite slowly. He seems to be a very old Gingoile. Even older than Medwick, with a distinct silver/grey moustache. 'Nurf inj pok yurtle brauw.'

What!? The "good morning, everyone" was slow but perfectly understandable. What on Earth, or indeed, what in The Realm, does "nurf inj pok yurtle brauw" mean!?

'Dak,' replies Medwick.

"Dak?" What is "Dak?" Have I gone back to sleep and am I now dreaming?

'Sorry, everyone,' says Medwick, 'Professor Krunk finds English quite difficult to speak. He was asking me to check with you if you don't mind him speaking slowly. Is that ok?'

'Of course, it is,' I reply 'but what language were you two just speaking?'

'Oh, that was Gingoilian. Only the older Gingoiles use it.'

'Do the Thargs have their own language?' asks Liz.

'Oh, yes,' replies Medwick, 'Thargassian. But when two Thargs have a conversation in it, it usually ends up in them fighting!'

'Why?' asks Carrot.

'Because they all have slightly different dialects. A word said with a slightly different accent can sound like a different word, possibly an offensive word, and rather than work it out sensibly, Thargs being Thargs they start hitting each other!

Interesting.

'Why was Zendorf speaking English from the hologram,' questions Carrot, 'rather than Thargassian or Gingoilian?'

Good question!

'Well,' replies Medwick, 'possibly partly due to more Gingoiles being able to understand English, since our ruler is English, than Thargassian; and he wanted to have as big an impact as possible. Or, possibly, down to the fact that I told him a long time ago that if he ever wants me to listen to him he needs to speak in Gingoilian or English. He refuses to speak Gingoilian, just like I refuse to speak Thargassian, so it forces him into English!'

I think I can see a slightly smug grin appearing under Medwick's moustache!

'Anyway,' continues Medwick, 'Professor Krunk has some news.'

'Yes,' says the Professor taking a step forwards, 'I have been studying the device for the past seven hours.' Blimey! I feel guilty for having such a good night's sleep! 'And about half an hour ago I discovered that the holographic transmitter contains two signals. The main signal transmitted the holographic image of Zendorf. The secondary signal was hidden on a harmonic oscillating frequency. Due to this the image is poor, but this is what I found.' Harmonic what? Oh well, as long as he's discovered something! He prods a screwdriver into the transmitter and places it on the table in front of us.

'Hello! Is this thing working? I'm afraid I'm a bit rusty!' says a voice from the transmitter.

'Mark! It's Uncle Mark!' exclaims Liz.

I'm not sure. At the moment there is only a voice coming from the device.

'Is there an image, Krunk?' asks Medwick.

'It comes,' replies the Professor.

'Hang on,' says the transmitter voice, 'I think that adjusting this should help...' a faded image appears. It is about one foot high and being beamed only about six inches away from the transmitter.

'See!' shouts Liz excitedly. 'It is Uncle Mark.' Is it?

'Is it? I've seen photos of him, Liz, but he never looked like that!' He is thin. His hair is long. He has a beard that is almost as long and a moustache that would challenge a Gingoile's for length!

'He's in prison. The Thargs aren't looking after him. But it is him, isn't it Medwick?' adds Liz.

Medwick stares at the image.

'It is him. It is your uncle. It is The Ruler of The Realm,' answers Medwick as he bows his head towards the image. Herf and the Professor follow suit.

'Now then,' continues Uncle Mark, 'if I've got this right, then you've spotted the deliberate mistake I made wlth Zendorf's size and one of you clever old Gingoiles, probably Krunk, has managed to access my harmonic oscillating frequency.'

The Professor smiles a smug moustache covered smile.

'I'm guessing Medwick and Herf are watching this and hoping, if I've managed to keep count of the days correctly, that my nephew, Eddie, is with you. The reason I've made this message is to tell you not to rescue me, but rescue the formula. If you rescue me, I won't have a Realm to rule over as my Gingoiles will still die. Rescue the formula, save the Gingoiles and even if I die, Eddie will become The Ruler of The Realm. Because my death is a possibility, I instruct you all to take care of Eddie. Also, rescuing me first will just make the Thargs increase the security around the formula and we'll never retrieve it. I am in the North Tower of The Dark Castle. I don't know where the formula is; but I assume it is in one of the other towers. I've got to go now. A guard is due to look in on me in a minute. Good luck. Goodbye.' The image fades. All is quiet apart from a snivel coming from Liz.

'Poor Uncle Mark,' sobs Liz, 'what have they done to him?'

'All that effort,' says Carrot, 'just to tell us not to save him!'

There's a pause. I don't know what to say. How can I not save my own uncle?

'We can't just leave him there,' says Becky, 'we've come here to save him, haven't we?'

Not for the first time, all eyes are on me. I hate that. The pressure!

'Uncle Mark doesn't want us to not save him,' I say. 'He just wants us to save the formula first.'

'But,' says Liz with tears welling up in her eyes, 'if we save the formula first, then the Thargs will increase the security around Uncle Mark. We can only save one.'

She's got a point. Based on what Uncle Mark has said, whichever one we save first will make it harder to save the second due to increased security.

'Then we save them both at the same time!' I say.

'How, Eddie,' asks Carrot, 'they're locked away in different towers?'

'We'll split up,' I announce.

'There's thousands of Thargs, Bro, how can three of us save one and only two of us save the other?'

Oh, I don't know! I'm just trying to be positive.

'We could do it, couldn't we, Medwick?' I plead.

Medwick looks at us all, one at a time, smiling warmly with his eyes.

'Master Eddie, you and your friends are indeed very brave. But,' he says, looking only at me now, 'the scroll that Herf read from when we first met told you that there needed to be five, six or seven of you if you are to have a chance of succeeding. That scroll was an ancient scroll written with direct reference to the saving of The Ruler, if he was ever a captive. It was written with regards to saving only one thing. You have the correct numbers to attempt saving one thing, and only one thing. That's not to say you can't try and save a second thing afterwards, but I strongly recommend you remain as a group and do not split up. You already know the potential downside of splitting up.'

'So,' I say whilst still absorbing what Medwick has just said, 'which one should I save first?'

'That, Master Eddie, has been told to you by The Ruler. You are his nephew and heir. Not one of his subjects. You may choose not to do as your Uncle Mark says. But, as one of his subjects, what he said was a command. I would save the formula first.'

'So, you would save your own neck before my uncle's?' blurts out Liz.

'Steady on, Sis,' I say.

'But that's what he's saying, isn't he? Save the formula, save the Gingoiles, let Uncle Mark be killed!' Liz can't hold the tears back any longer.

'And Eddie will become The Ruler of The Realm and de-throne Zendorf,' replies Medwick.

'But Uncle Mark will still die!' screams Liz.

'Calm down, Liz,' says Becky putting a consoling arm around her shoulder.

'Who says anything about dying or killing?' asks Medwick, 'I said try and save the formula first. That's all.'

'They may just increase the security around your uncle,' says Carrot, 'then we come away, regroup and try and save him. I think what your uncle really meant was for us not to try and save them both at the same time, or one straight after the other. Save the formula, save the Gingoiles, let things cool off a bit and then try to save your uncle when the security starts to lapse again.'

Wow, Carrot. Not a pizza monster in sight!

'I think a member of your team has just hit the nail on the head,' says Medwick, 'don't you, Master Eddie?'

Eyes, once more, are uncomfortably upon me. I choose not to speak, but think. No one interrupts me for quite a while.

'Well, Eddie?' rasps Liz, eventually. 'The Gingoiles or our uncle? Which do you want us to attempt to save?' Carrot, Medwick, Herf and Krunk shake their heads at Liz's questions.

'Liz,' I say as warmly as I can, 'it's not a question of who I want to save. It's a question of who I need to save first.' I intend to continue after drawing breath, but I can't.

'Whoever you leave until second is gonna have to wait a long time before we can attempt to rescue them,' interrupts Liz, 'if we do what Carrot suggests.' True. 'Are you happy to leave Uncle Mark locked up for even longer whilst you save the formula? He's been in prison for ten years and not committed a crime! You gonna be responsible for leaving him in there longer just for the sake of a formula?'

I turn to face our Gingoile friends. 'Medwick,' I ask, 'if we rescue Uncle Mark first and, say, wait a year before attempting to rescue the formula, what will happen to the Gingoiles?'

'Approximately 7,000 of us will die of old age and seeing as we can't reproduce, there will be 7,000 less Gingoiles in The Realm and we will be 7,000 nearer to extinction as a race,' is Medwick's rather frank reply.

'If we save the formula first and leave Uncle Mark's rescue for a year, what will happen to your race?'

'Well,' replies Medwick, 'the 7,000 will obviously still die, but with the formula in our hands we will be able to reproduce and seeing as we have not had young for over 100 years, I dare say there will be what you call a "baby boom" or what we call a "Goiley boom"! We'll probably have 10-15,000 young Gingoiles within the year.'

I turn to Liz. 'You know that I intend to save the formula first. Uncle Mark wants us to and Medwick's explanation backs up my decision.'

'And you'll watch your uncle die?' says Liz with tears trickling down her face.

'Why do you think Uncle Mark will suddenly die?' I ask.

'They're bound to say "give us the formula back or we'll kill your uncle", aren't they?' replies Liz.

Are they? I hope not!

'They probably will say that,' says Medwick. Great! 'But they won't do it.'

'What makes you so sure?' asks Carrot.

'Well,' continues Medwick, 'they have kept your uncle prisoner for ten years so that there are no rightful rulers wandering The Realm looking to overthrow Zendorf. At the moment they have The Ruler of The Realm a captive. If they kill him, they will lose any kind of power they have because they will have set The Ruler free!'

'I don't really follow,' says Becky.

'Nor do I,' adds Brian.

'If they kill your uncle, then The Ruler of The Realm will be wandering The Realm once more. Eddie will become The Ruler and be free. With your uncle alive Zendorf controls The Ruler. With him dead he does not. He will not kill your uncle. He will be his only bargaining tool.'

Wow. This is getting really quite heavy.

'Do you promise that we'll attempt to rescue Uncle Mark after we've rescued the formula?' asks Liz.

'Of course,' I reply, 'we've just got to take our time and do one thing at a time.'

'We might as well take our time seeing as everything we do here will only last six seconds at home!' says Becky.

True.

'Why is your Ruler always a human and not a Gingoile? asks Brian, quite out of the blue.

Now that is a very good question!

'Where did that very good question come from, Brian?' I ask.

'Dunno,' he replies, 'just something that's been bothering me!'

We all turn to Medwick.

'Congratulations, Master Brian,' replies Medwick, 'one question I have been waiting for, but alas the answer to this will have to wait. Suffice to say that they haven't always been human. I will elaborate at a later date. For now, we need to get you on your way. You have a formula that needs rescuing!'

# Chapter Ten

'Now, then,' bustles Herf, 'your knapsacks are full and seeing as you know about the transportation zones, you're bound to have more than enough to eat on your journey.'

'Thanks, Herf,' I reply.

'If Uncle Mark is in the North Tower,' asks Liz, 'which tower would you think the formula is in?'

'Well,' replies Medwick, 'as you approach The Dark Castle the main entrance is through the South Tower, so I doubt it is there. The North Tower is the tallest tower, furthest away from you. The East Tower is to the right and the West Tower to the left. If your uncle is correct in his assumption, then it is probably in the East or West Tower. He may be completely wrong.' Great. 'All I'm going to say is that from now on everything may not be quite as it seems.'

'What does that mean?' asks Becky. I think we were all going to ask that one.

'Just be extra careful between here and The Dark Castle,' replies Medwick. 'Remember that you are not at home. The Realm holds many secrets. Everything may not be quite as it seems.'

He's said it again. It sounded spookier that time as well!

'So, the zone that takes us towards The Dark Castle is just down the hill at the back of the Palace?' asks Carrot, who seems eager to be on his way.

'Yes,' replies Medwick, 'the zone at the front of the Palace is back to the cave and the zone at the back is to the waterfall.'

'And the zones continue to follow the pattern round the edge of Eddie's box, do they?' asks Liz.

'More or less,' replies Medwick. 'Don't ask me to elaborate on that answer. Remember, you do need to discover things for yourself. Many things you discover and learn on your way to The Dark Castle will help you when you get there.'

'Can I just say one thing, Medwick?' asks Herf.

'If you must,' replies Medwick, 'but no clues!'

94

'Oh, it isn't really a clue,' continues Herf, 'just to say that the waterfall is very noisy and slippery.'

Medwick raises his eyes upwards.

'Thanks for that,' says Becky giving Herf a hug.

Herf bows his head slightly to cover up his embarrassment.

'I guess you're not coming down to the zone to see us off, then?' I ask.

'No,' replies Medwick, 'we'll see you off from here.'

I thought he'd say that.

'Will we see you again?' asks Liz.

'Oh, yes,' replies Medwick, 'we'll all see each other again some time.'

\*

We're on our way down the hill to the zone. The goodbyes were briefer this time. They were dragged out the first time we left Medwick 'coz we felt like we weren't going to see him and Herf again; or at least not for a long time. Now we all know that he could pop up anywhere! I still don't fully understand why he won't help us more? We'd better learn some huge lessons from discovering everything ourselves otherwise I'm going to get quite annoyed!

'Here's the zone!' says Carrot who's been brave enough to take point once more. 'Shall I go first?'

'It's up to you,' I reply.

Although he's appearing brave, I don't want to force him in any way.

'I don't mind going first,' says Becky.

'Nor me!' add Brian and Liz, virtually simultaneously.

We all stop and laugh. My group of misfits is starting to turn into a team.

'Ok,' I say, 'seeing as you asked first, you can lead, Carrot.'

'Ok, Eddie.'

'We'll do the same as before. We'll give you 30 seconds to get off the zone and come back if there's a problem. Once 30 seconds has passed one of us will join you. Ok?'

'Fine,' replies Carrot.

'And mind your step, Carrot,' says Liz, 'remember that Herf said it was slippery.'

'And noisy!' adds Becky.

'It's ok, I'll be fine!' replies a slightly impatient sounding Carrot.

If we are not careful, and keep going on, Carrot will lose his nerve and back out of taking the lead.

'Right, I'm off,' announces Carrot, seemingly gathering his nerve again. 'See you in 30 seconds!'

He steps onto the zone, lifts his arm as if he's going to wave, but before he can he's gone.

'Shall I go next, Bro?'

'Guess so,' I reply looking at my watch. 'Thirty secs almost up; take care, Sis.'

I smile at Liz who is still smiling in return as she steps onto the zone and disappears.

'You next, Eddie,' says Brian, 'then Becky, and I'll come last.'

'Sounds ok with me,' I say. 'Is that ok with you, Becky?'

'Fine,' she replies.

'Ok, time's up! I'm going!' I say as I step onto the zone and... Wow! The noise. The light display dazzling through the waterfall which is about 20 feet away from me and... Whoaaa! The slippery floor as I step off the zone.

'Careful, Bro!' says Liz as both she and Carrot stop me from falling completely into the shallow water which surrounds the zone.

'Thanks, Liz,' I say. 'Thanks, Carrot.'

'No problem,' says Carrot.

'Anything to report?' I add.

'Just that the ground's very slippery!' laughs Carrot.

Ha, ha, very funny!

'What's funny?' says Becky who's appeared on the zone.

'Herf's right, Becky,' says Liz, 'the ground is very slippery. The heir here,' she pokes me lightly with a finger, 'would've fallen over if me and Carrot hadn't caught him!'

Becky giggles as she steps gingerly off the zone and over to us.

'Ok,' I say, 'joke's over. Can we not tell Brian? His guffawing might notify any passing Thargs. Even over the sound of this waterfall!'

'Ok,' they all say.

'Cool!' booms the voice of Brian behind us. 'I like this!'

He's looking at the light refracting around the cave behind the waterfall. We're not really looking at what he's looking at. We're all looking at his feet as he steps off the zone... Nothing! No slip; nothing. He's either got very good soles on his shoes or his extra weight means that he grips better! We all exchange glances. I guess we're all thinking the same!

'Right!' continues Brian. 'Where to now?'

Where indeed?

'Well,' says Carrot, 'I've been looking around for a zone with a mountain on; it is the mountain next isn't it, Eddie?' I take out the box to double-check.

'Yes,' I reply, 'mountain, then lake.'

'No other zone in here,' continues Carrot, 'must be another waterfall with a zone in around here somewhere.'

'How do we get out?' asks Becky.

We all look around. Nothing but damp cave behind a raging waterfall.

'Can't see anything,' says Liz. 'How about you, Brian?'

Of course, Brian. Our King of Senses! He looks around slowly.

'I think there's a ledge going round the corner there,' says Brian, pointing to the edge of the cave as it disappears behind the waterfall. I think he's right. 'I'll go and look!' Brian strides off. Without slipping! Amazing!!

'Yep,' he announces, 'the ledge here goes behind the waterfall and to another opening just along a bit.'

Just along a bit. That sounds really accurate!

'Well done, Brian,' says Becky throwing him a smile.

'Better be careful with your footing,' says Liz as she carefully heads towards Brian, 'we don't want you to slip, Eddie, do we!?'

She laughs as she says this. So do Carrot and Becky. Luckily Brian is looking down the ledge and he's too close to the noisy waterfall to hear them.

We all tread carefully as we venture to join Brian by the ledge.

'That's just along a bit, is it?' asks Carrot of Brian.

'Well,' says Brian, 'I was gonna make a guess at the distance, but I would have guessed in metres and you lot seem to only work in feet and inches!'

Carrot and I chuckle. I don't think Liz and Becky quite get the joke.

'Well,' I say, 'it looks like 20 feet.'

'It's not that measurement I'm concerned about,' says Carrot, 'it's more the width of the ledge.'

We all glance down. It doesn't look much wider than the beam we use in PE at school. About four or five inches in places.

'It's ok,' I say pointing to the cliff face above the ledge, 'there are plenty of hand holds.'

Everyone looks up. I don't think they are convinced.

'Do you have a rope in one of your pockets, Carrot?' asks Liz.

Carrot starts to pat his pockets. It's starting to look like some sort of tribal dance! He can't surely have a rope concealed on his person, can he?

'Not a rope, as such,' replies Carrot whilst continuing to do his patting pocket dance, 'but a... oh, here it is!'

Carrot pulls what looks like string from one of his many pockets.

'String?' says Becky.

'No,' replies Carrot looking at Becky rather disgusted at her suggestion, 'it's extra strong, extra light nylon thread. Can hold the weight of ten grown men!'

'Tried it, have you?' asks Liz.

'No, that's just what it said on the packet.'

Pause. Carrot looks a bit upset by the jibes.

'You did ask for rope, Sis. This nylon stuff is better than nothing. I'm surprised we've found anything between us! What do you want to do with it?'

'You're right, Eddie, sorry Carrot,' Carrot nods acknowledgement of the apology. 'I thought that Brian could go across first, with the rope tied this end, and he could tie the other end so that we have a rope handrail.'

'How does that sound?' I ask of everyone.

'Ok,' say Brian and Becky.

'Well,' says Carrot, 'it sounds ok, but if we slip and lose our hand grip then that's it!' Nicely put, Carrot. 'But if we do what mountaineers do and tie the rope to each of us as well as Brian tying at the far end then we should be ok.'

Should be, I guess!

'That sounds better,' say Becky and Liz.

'Ok everyone,' I announce, 'tie on nice and tight. Give Brian lots of slack so he can make it across before we set off.' Everyone fumbles to tie the rope around their waists. I let Carrot sort everyone out. After all, it is his nylony ropey stuff! I take my box out of my pocket. There's a slight glow on the waterfall symbol. Hopefully that means we're going to head down the correct ledge and there isn't another way out of here. The next symbol is a mountain, then a lake and then a castle. Presumably The Dark Castle. As long as not all the zones are as tricky as this one, we should be there soon. I'm not sure if that's good or bad!

'Ok, Eddie,' says Carrot, 'all secure and ready to go!'

'Thanks Carrot,' I reply.

'Brian first, then Becky, then you, Eddie, then Liz and me,' continues Carrot.

'Ok,' we all say.

'Right,' says Brian, 'off we go!'

He edges himself along the ledge, holding small crevices on the cliff face with the rope dangling down from his belt. He's making it look easy, but we all know his shoes have the best grip. Twenty feet doesn't seem to take him more than 30 seconds.

'Well done,' shouts Liz. Brian waves and starts to tie the rope to a jutting-out rock. I don't think he can hear us over the noise of the waterfall.

'Ok, Becky,' I say, 'your turn. Take it steady. You don't have to go as quick as Brian. No rush! Remember everything we do here only lasts six seconds at home!'

'Ok, Eddie,' replies Becky with a smile.

She starts to edge along the ledge, gets about halfway and stops where the ledge is at its narrowest.

'You ok?' shouts Liz. No reply.

'She can't hear you over the water,' I say to Liz. 'I'll try. Are you ok?' I bellow.

She must have heard that. Apparently not!

'What's Brian doing?' says Carrot. Brian is gesticulating towards Becky.

'I think he's trying to urge her on,' says Liz. 'I think she's having a panic attack and has frozen to the spot.'

'Shall I go after her?' asks Carrot.

'I don't think so,' I say, 'that might make matters worse.'

Just then Becky starts to edge forward again. Then, before any of us can cheer her on, she slips and we find ourselves being tugged forward by her weight pulling us. Carrot, Liz and I all grab at the rocks and adjust our footing so as to prevent Becky from slipping any further, but she has gone over the edge and is dangling from her waist. Her screams are so loud that we can hear them over the waterfall.

'Take her weight,' screams Liz.

'Stand still,' hollers Carrot.

'I am,' I say as I find myself at the front of this trio being slowly dragged inch by inch towards the edge by the dangling Becky.

We look along the narrow walkway wondering what to do next when we see Brian edging back along the path to Becky. He's no longer connected to the rope since he tied it to the rock.

'Brian,' shouts Carrot, 'go back! You're not tied on to anyone or anything!'

Brian probably can't hear Carrot; but even if he could I doubt if he'd take any notice of him. Brian gets close to where Becky is dangling and goes down on to one knee. He pulls on the rope with one hand and lunges down with his other hand to grab Becky's flailing outstretched fingers. His shoes remain stuck to the wet surface like limpets as he slowly pulls Becky to the ledge. The three of us sigh an audible sigh of relief as the strain is taken off the nylony stuff and Brian leads Becky to the other side. We peer through the water mist at the other two. Brian has his arm round Becky's shoulder. He looks at us and gives us the thumbs up. I guess that means it's my turn to go.

'Take care, Bro,' says Liz.

'Be careful, mate,' adds Carrot.

'I will,' is my tentative reply as I decide to focus on Brian and Becky and not look down at my feet. Instead, I choose to push my foot right up against the cliff face with every step. This seems to work and it's not long before I join Brian and Becky. I turn and wave at Liz who immediately sets off. She takes it steady and seems to have adopted a similar approach to me with her feet. I turn to Becky and ask her if she's ok.

'I couldn't move,' she says. 'Brian got me to focus and move on, but as I did my legs turned to jelly and I slipped.' Liz and Carrot have now joined us.

'Well done Brian!' says Liz.

'Thanks,' replies Brian.

'It was a bit silly, though, Brian,' interjects Carrot, 'you weren't attached to anything or anyone.'

'I know,' says Brian, 'but I only thought about that on the way back. It was silly, but I had to do something!'

He throws a sheepish smile towards Becky.

'Silly, but very brave,' says Carrot.

'Thanks, Carrot,' replies Brian.

Well said Carrot. It was both silly and brave. They do tend to go hand in hand, don't they?

'Ok,' I say as Carrot collects his nylony stuff and replaces it into some hidden pocket. 'Are we all ok then?'

I aim this comment mostly at Becky.

'Yes,' they all reply.

'Right, let's find that other zone then!'

We all trudge slowly into the cave, away from the cascading water.

'What's this?' cries out Liz who's standing near the wall of the cave. We gather around her. In front of us is what looks like a nest covered with lots of feathers and entwined limbs.

'Looks like dead swans,' says Brian.

'Must be Aycks,' joins in Becky.

'Oh yes,' says Carrot, 'it was Ayck feathers which we had in our duvets at the Palace, wasn't it?'

'Yes,' I reply, 'and Herf told me they were like swans with really long necks.'

We all look down at the mass of feathers once more. There are definitely a lot of entwined limbs, including what looks like two very long necks.

'Who would do this?' says Becky.

'Thargs?' questions Brian.

'Maybe,' I say, 'but why?'

'Maybe they don't like anything in The Realm other than Thargs,' says Carrot.

Maybe.

'If these two Aycks are on a nest, maybe there are eggs underneath them?' suggests Liz.

'Ah,' blurts out Carrot, 'maybe that's why they were killed; so that the eggs could be taken!'

'Maybe,' I say once more. 'There's only one way of finding out!' I look round the team. 'Who's gonna help me lift them to check underneath for any eggs?'

'I will,' says Brian striding forward with his shoes still gripping the moist rocks as if it's a bone-dry surface.

'Do it gently,' says Becky.

'We will,' replies Brian whilst flashing another smile towards Becky.

I start to put my hands in between the two bodies. Brian gets the idea and gently starts to pull one to one side so that I can get my hands into the middle of the nest. I feel around and find my fingers touching something smooth. Something quite large, quite warm and smooth.

'I've got something,' I say as I gently pull out a large Ayck egg.

It's yellow in colour with a pink hue.

'They obviously didn't want the egg!' says Liz.

'Maybe they didn't want to eat the egg,' adds Becky, 'maybe they just didn't want the baby Ayck to be born?'

'Is it still warm?' Liz asks me.

I can feel some warmth in my hands.

'Quite warm,' I reply.

'These big Aycks aren't cold yet, either,' adds Brian.

'Then we should keep the Ayck egg warm,' says Becky.

'And take it with us!?' questions Carrot.

'Yes!' replies Becky.

'Where are you going to keep it?' asks Liz. 'It's quite large.'

Becky takes off her knapsack and takes the egg from me.

'In here,' says Becky, pointing into her open bag.

'Are you sure?' I ask.

I mean, carrying an egg the size of a rugby ball, in your backpack and into a potential battle can't be right, can it?

'I'll wrap it up warm. You never know, it might hatch,' says Becky.

'And then what?' asks Carrot.

'Well,' continues Becky as she is doing up her knapsack, 'I'm wondering why the Thargs killed these Aycks whilst they were defenceless on their nest and left the egg to go cold?'

'Because they're horrible?' offers Carrot.

'Maybe,' replies Becky, 'or maybe they are scared of Aycks, and the only time they can kill them is when they are nesting.'

Interesting thought!

'Why on earth would Thargs be scared of long-necked swans?' asks Carrot.

'I don't know,' replies Becky, 'it's just a thought. After all, Medwick did say that everything might not be quite as it seems. And I don't want this baby Ayck to die if I can give it a chance of life.'

Sounds fine by me.

'Is that ok, Eddie?' asks Becky.

'Sure,' I say, 'if you're happy carrying it, it's fine by me. And you never know; you might be right about the Thargs not liking them. There's certainly something a bit odd about these Aycks.'

'I've found it.' We all look up. It's Brian from the back of the cave. 'A zone with a mountain on it,' he says.

'Well done, Brian,' offers Liz.

'Great work,' I add as we trudge towards Brian who's standing by a zone just like all the others, but with a picture of a mountain on it.

'Want me to go first?' asks Brian.

'If you want to, Brian,' I reply.

'Ok,' he says, 'see you in 30 seconds!' And he steps on the zone and disappears.

'No stopping him now, is there Bro!?' laughs Liz.

'No!' I say. 'Want to go next, Sis?'

'Ok,' she replies.

'Thirty seconds up,' interjects Carrot who is intently watching his watch.'

'Right,' says Liz, 'guess it's all clear! See you soon!' She follows Brian.

'You next Eddie,' says Carrot.

'Ok,' I reply. 'You bringing up the rear, Carrot?'

'Sure am! Ok, time to go Eddie.'

'Right,' I say, 'see you two shortly.' I step onto the zone and here we go again...............

# Chapter Eleven

Good grief! It's freezing!

'Over here!' calls out Liz who is, and I never thought I'd say this, huddled up against Brian!

'What are you doing?' I ask.

'Keeping warm!' is her obvious reply. 'Any other ideas of how to do that?'

'No,' I say.

'Get in here then!' says Liz grabbing me.

'Can I join in?' says Becky stepping off the zone behind me.

'Of course,' says Brian.

Liz and I throw him knowing stares.

'Just Carrot and we'll have a complete scrum,' I say, trying to keep the spirits up.

Brian's arms seem to stretch around all three of us!

'Room for one more?' says Carrot approaching. He squeezes in between me and Becky.

'When your box showed a picture of a mountain, did it really have to be near the top of a snow-covered mountain!?' says Liz.

'Sorry,' I say, 'the picture on the box isn't very clear. The key is finding the next zone, with a picture of a lake on it, as soon as possible.'

'Oh, don't worry about that,' says Liz, 'Brian found that straight away!'

'Really, Brian,' I say, 'where is it?'

'Round the corner,' replies Brian.

'So, why are we all standing here freezing?' asks Carrot who seems to be developing an icicle on the end of his nose.

''Coz there's a slight problem,' continues Brian.

'What sort of problem?' I ask.

'Something's in the way,' says Brian.

'What's in the way?' asks Becky.

'Can't describe them really,' explains Brian. 'Some sort of group of snow monkeys with bright green eyes!'

'Did that last transportation zone affect you, or something?' says Carrot, chuckling.

'No,' replies a disgruntled Brian, 'take a look yourself, but don't get too close to them.'

'Why not?' I ask.

''Coz when I moved towards the zone, which was quite near to them, they started to get tense and their eyes turned yellow!'

'Yellow?' says Becky.

'Yes,' replies Brian, 'so I thought I'd come back here and wait for you lot.'

'Good thinking, Brian,' I say. 'I suppose we should go and take a look at these monkeys before we decide what to do next. Lead on Brian.'

'Just round here,' says Brian leading us no more than twenty feet round a corner.

There, in front of us, just as Brian described, are what appear to be snow monkeys. Eight of them. With piercing green eyes.

'They're beautiful,' whispers Becky.

'You can't put one of them in your knapsack along with the egg, Becky!' says Liz, smiling.

'No need,' replies Becky, 'they look like a happy family.'

'You sure they started to become threatening when you moved towards them, Brian?' I ask.

'Yes, want me to show you?'

'Ok,' I reply, 'if you're sure. But don't get too close.'

Brian slowly walks towards them and initially the monkeys take no notice and continue to play amongst themselves. Then one or two start to look at Brian and their eyes turn yellow.

'Ok, Brian,' I say in a raised whisper, 'I think you should come back now.'

Brian puts his hand up in acknowledgement, but keeps on edging towards the monkeys. All the monkeys are backing away from Brian, all with bright yellow eyes.

'Brian,' says Liz in a louder voice than me, 'come back now.'

Brian waves his hand again. I look at Liz who glances back at me. Brian takes two more steps and suddenly all eight monkeys are in a row facing Brian with their now orange eyes gleaming. As a unit they all stand up on their hind legs facing Brian.

'Please stop, Brian!' cries out Becky from beside me.

Brian pauses and walks slowly backwards away from the monkeys, keeping his eyes on them at all times. As he returns, the monkeys start to relax and their eyes return to green via yellow. Brian returns to us as the monkeys are playing again as if nothing had happened.

'Why didn't you come back when we called?' asks Liz.

That's what I was thinking.

'I just wanted to see whether they would run away!' replies Brian.

'I don't think they were going to, Brian,' I say.

'They were impressive, weren't they?' says Liz. 'Like soldiers.'

'They did look organised,' says Becky.

'Red!' says Carrot.

'You what?' I reply.

'Red!' he repeats. 'Their eyes went from green to yellow and then to orange.'

'And?' asks Liz.

'And they were about to attack, so I think their eyes were going to go to red next.'

'Why red?' I ask.

'The colours of the rainbow!' is Carrot's reply.

'I still don't follow,' says Liz.

'Green,' begins Carrot, 'is the central colour of the rainbow. There are three colours each side of it. As the monkeys become more agitated, they go to yellow. Then they become organised and aggressive on orange and I think they would attack on red. Red for danger!'

'But red might not mean danger here, Carrot,' offers Becky.

'No. But it might.'

'How is working that out going to get us past them?' asks Liz. 'I don't want them to go red and attack us just to prove your theory!'

'No,' says Carrot, only slightly miffed from the rebuff. 'But if my theory is right, then we need to get their eyes to go to blue, indigo and violet to get them docile enough to get past!'

Interesting.

'Ok,' I say, 'any suggestions on how to keep the rainbow-eyed snow monkeys nearer purple than red?'

The others smile cold smiles.

'Food!' says Brian.

'Good idea, Brian,' I say. 'Finding food amongst all this snow can't be easy. What have we got?'

We all start to look in our knapsacks.

'Sandwiches,' says Carrot.

'Some sort of fruit,' says Becky.

'Me too,' adds Liz.

'A flan,' says Brian.

'I seem to have some strange broccoli stuff!' I announce.

'Now what?' says Carrot.

'Shall I take it nearer to them and throw it towards them?' asks Brian.

'Yes,' I reply, 'but show it to them first to see if they are interested and to see if their eyes change colour.'

'Hopefully to blue and not yellow!' adds Liz.

'Ok,' says Brian as he picks up the food and shoves it into his pockets as he sets off towards the monkeys once more.

'Good luck,' calls out Becky.

Liz and I exchange our glances once more. Brian walks towards the monkeys and stops as they look up at him and their eyes change to yellow. He takes a sandwich from one pocket and some of my broccoli stuff from another and holds it up. The monkey's eyes immediately return to green.

'Amazing,' says Becky. Brian squats down whilst still holding out the food. The monkeys also squat down as their eyes turn to blue.

'Incredible,' says Liz. 'It looks like you're right, Carrot!'

Carrot beams. Brian throws the sandwich towards one of the monkeys who is squatting like an obedient pet. The monkey stretches out a long arm and picks up the sandwich. As he does so, his eyes turn to indigo. Brian carefully throws a piece of food to all the other monkeys who are squatting quietly, waiting their turn. All their eyes turn to indigo, too.

'This is just unbelievable,' I find myself saying aloud.

Brian sits down. The monkeys copy him. Brian puts the rest of the food in a pile in front of the semi-circle of monkeys. Their eyes turn to what can only be described as violet. Brian turns towards us and gesticulates to come past but keep down low.

'What's he want us to do?' asks Carrot.

'Crawl past him to the zone,' I say. 'I think that they may find walking intimidating.'

'I'll lead,' says Liz.

We all follow on all fours. The snow is freezing on both hands and knees. The monkeys only glance at us with their beautiful violet eyes as we crawl slowly past. Brian joins the end of our strange procession.

'Well done, Brian,' I say, 'great job! Now let's get on this zone to the lake before they finish the food.'

'Good thinking,' says Carrot, 'I'll go first.' He crawls onto the zone and disappears.

'I think his working out the rainbow eyes has given Carrot a new lease of bravery!' says Liz.

'I agree,' I reply. 'Time's up! You next, Becky.'

'Ok.'

'You bringing up the rear Brian?' I ask.

'Yes,' he replies, 'but can we hurry up? The monkeys are finishing the food!'

I turn around. The monkeys are picking up the last few crumbs and their eyes are back to blue.

'Ok,' I say, 'I'm going. Just give me and Liz twenty seconds ok, Brian?'

'Sure,' says Brian looking nervously over his shoulder.

'Ok,' I say. 'See you at the lake!'

*

At last; warmth! A beautiful lake which is as still as a millpond surrounded by trees. Eight Aycks swimming around somewhere near the centre of the lake. Becky and Carrot are sitting down close by, looking as if they are enjoying the warmth as much as I am.

'Nice, isn't it, mate!?' says Carrot.

'It's more than nice!' I reply.

'And warm!' joins in Liz who has just stepped off the zone.

'I hope Brian makes it,' I say.

'Why? What's wrong?' asks Becky hurriedly.

'The monkeys were running out of food as I left,' continues Liz. 'Their eyes were back to green.'

'Here he is!' says Carrot.

'You alright, Brian?' I ask.

He looks a bit flustered.

'Their eyes were up to yellow when I left,' blurts out Brian. 'I think we should move from here.'

'Why?' asks Carrot.

''Coz I think they might be following us!'

Carrot and Becky immediately jump up from the ground.

'I'm sure they won't follow us, Brian,' I say.

'Why not?' asks Brian.

'Well,' I continue, 'first of all they weren't interested in following us on the mountain. They just became wary of us when we got close to them.'

'That's before we gave them food,' says Liz. 'They might be more interested in us now.'

I hadn't thought of that!

'That's true,' I continue. 'But, secondly, those monkeys looked like they belonged in the snow. They were happy. I'm sure it's too warm for them here.'

'You're probably right,' says Becky, 'but it's probably better if we move. Just in case!'

She's right!

'Ok,' I say, 'the next zone will have The Dark Castle on it. Can anyone see it?' We all start to look around.

'Seeing as we're getting closer to The Dark Castle,' says Liz, 'don't you think we should hide in the trees and be a bit more careful?'

'You're right,' I say, 'let's get into those trees quickly.'

I lead everyone under a nearby tree.

'Sorry,' I say, 'after being in the cold, where no one would be hanging around, and then getting away from the monkeys, I thought we could relax. I wasn't thinking straight.'

'That's ok,' says Carrot, 'me and Becky just sat down in the sun when we got here. We should have come into these trees straight away.'

'Never mind,' joins in Brian, 'we're here now and I can't see anyone, so I don't think anyone has seen us.'

Thank goodness!

'Where do you reckon the next zone is, Bro?'

'Seeing as the only picture on my box is a lake,' I reply whilst studying my box again, 'then I guess it is around the edge of the lake somewhere.' We all look out towards the lake which now, suddenly, seems bigger with the prospect of possibly walking around it.

'Shall we split up?' asks Carrot. 'Three one way, two the other? We'll find the zone quicker that way!'

'We've split up before,' I reply, 'and we all know what happened that time, don't we?'

Knowing nods are aimed in my direction.

'So, we'll stick together then,' I add. 'Which way shall we go, Brian? Can you see any clues?'

Brian has a good look around.

'There's no wind!' comes Brian's strange reply.

I look around. He's right. The others look at Brian and me rather bemused!

'Fair enough, Brian,' I say, 'but what has that got to do with the zone?'

'I don't know what it's got to do with the zone,' continues Brian, 'but there are two trees on the opposite side of the lake whose leaves are moving. None of the leaves on any other tree are moving at all!'

He's right. Just those two trees.

'Spooky!' says Becky.

'Very!' adds Liz.

'They're actually moving now!' says Carrot excitedly.

'That's what I said,' replies Brian.

'No,' continues Carrot, 'I don't just mean moving, as in swaying in the wind, I mean the leaves are actually moving around the branches!'

'Good grief,' I say, 'you're right, Carrot!'

The leaves *are* moving.

'They're making a shape,' says Brian.

They are. I cannot believe we're standing, watching leaves moving around a tree!

'Two arrows,' continues Brian, 'pointing down towards the ground in between the two trees.'

'The zone?' asks Becky.

'Must be,' answers Liz.

'Or a trap,' says Carrot. They all look at me.

'I don't know,' I say, in a very un-leader-like voice! 'I guess we slowly make our way towards it, keeping under the trees and bushes, and see what it looks like from a bit closer.'

There we go. Decision made!

'Ok,' says Brian, 'shall I lead?'

'Sure,' I say, 'you seem to have the best eyesight.'

Brian goes off, followed by Becky, then me, Liz and Carrot.

'Take us close enough for you to see more,' I say in a hushed voice to Brian, 'and maybe no more talking whilst we're moving.'

That sounded more leader-like!

This place is unbelievably amazing. On top of everything we have seen and done, now leaves are wandering around trees and making arrow shapes in their branches! Hang on. The Aycks are looking a bit restless. Brian stops and squats down. We all copy him.

'The arrows have gone,' Brian says. We all look up.

'They're moving into another shape,' points out Becky.

'It looks like "S and T" on the left tree,' says Liz, 'and "O and P" on the right tree.'

'"STOP,"' I say, 'it's telling us to stop!'

'But, why?' asks Liz.

'Maybe *this* is a trap?' says Carrot.

'Or maybe it's telling us to stop 'coz of him?' says Brian gingerly lifting a hand to point out a Tharg who is standing in between the two trees.

'I'm guessing he has just appeared on the zone,' I say.

'Now what?' asks Becky.

'Now we sit very quietly,' I reply, 'and see if your theory about Thargs not liking Aycks is true. Look at them!'

I point towards the Aycks who are heading towards the Tharg. Some of them are flapping their wings rather menacingly. The Tharg starts to walk in our direction. Towards the bush we are all hiding behind. I don't think he's seen us; I think he's just heading towards the other zone.

'What now?' asks Liz.

'I don't know,' I reply because I really just don't know!

Then the Aycks start to increase their flapping and start making a noise. A not unpleasant noise, but a strange noise. A "radio tuning into opera but not quite getting there" sort of noise. The Tharg immediately puts his double thumbed hands over his ears and starts talking to himself as if to try and block out the noise. A noise he clearly doesn't like. Then the few Aycks who haven't already started the noise join in. Much deeper. The bass section. Just like my grandpa who would practise his amateur operatics whilst cooking our tea. The noise is now becoming cacophonous. But not painful. At least not to us. But the Tharg is now in agony as he runs away from us and back on to the zone he arrived on. He's gone. The Aycks quieten down.

We all look at each other.

'Looks like I was right!' smiles Becky.

'It certainly does!' I reply.

Everyone starts to giggle.

'I didn't think it was that bad,' says Carrot.

'Compared to your taste in music,' I say, 'it wasn't bad!'

The laughter continues.

'Look,' says Brian stopping us all mid-giggle, 'the arrows have returned on the tree!'

We all look up once more. There they are again. Two big arrows pointing to the spot where the Tharg disappeared.

'Ok,' I say, 'we know where the zone is, but maybe we should give the Tharg a little time at the other end to move away before using it.'

'Sounds a good idea, Bro.'

'I agree,' join in Brian and Carrot.

'We don't know where exactly at The Dark Castle the zone is going to be, do we Eddie?' asks Becky.

'No,' I reply, 'why?'

'Well,' she continues, 'worrying about one Tharg might be the least of our problems. The zone might be near lots of Thargs, or it might be guarded. We could go on that zone one at a time and be captured one at a time as we appear at the other end.'

Erm. Oh dear.

'Any ideas?' I say meekly.

There's a pause. A pause which sounds like a pause which means "you work it out, you're the heir to the throne"!

'I don't have an idea,' says Brian, 'but they might!'

He points over my shoulder. I turn round swiftly and see Medwick and Herf making their way towards us from the mountain zone.

'I wondered when they might appear again!' says Liz.

'Same here!' I concur.

'Watch your back, Master Eddie, watch your back,' I can hear Medwick repeating as he approaches.

'I was,' I reply as Medwick comes nearer, 'or at least Brian was watching it for me!'

'Did you see us arrive?' asks Herf.

'Yes,' says Brian, 'and because I recognised you we didn't hide.'

'Very good,' says Medwick, 'very impressive vision indeed young Brian.' Brian smiles.

'Found the next zone?' enquires Medwick.

'Hang on,' I say, 'what are you doing here?'

A fair enough question I feel.

'Just seeing if you are all alright,' replies Medwick.

'We are now, no thanks to you,' I say.

Medwick and Herf seem slightly taken aback by my manner.

'What's wrong?' asks Medwick. 'You all look fine to me.'

'Where shall I begin?' I say. 'How about one of us nearly falling to our death in the waterfall, one of us being on the verge of an assault by a line of kung-fu fighting snow monkeys and all of us being put under the threat of a Tharg attack until the Aycks noisily rescued us. And that's not to mention the messages being sent from leaves!'

I point up to the two giant leaf arrows as I make my final point.

Medwick and Herf look up at the leaves.

'Aah,' says Medwick, 'the leaves are walking, Herf, the leaves are walking...'

'The leaves are walking,' murmurs Herf in imitation.

We wait for more words of wisdom.

'Well,' continues Medwick eventually, 'I did say that you would have to discover things for yourself and you have!'

'I know,' I reply, 'but a little help would have been appreciated.'

'But you achieved it all by yourselves,' says Medwick. 'Aren't you proud of yourselves?'

'I suppose we are,' answers Liz, 'if you put it like that. But some of us could have lost our lives.'

'I understand,' replies Medwick, 'but what you face at The Dark Castle will be much more dangerous than what you have already encountered.' Great! 'Just remember how you got through all your problems and look towards your discoveries to help you in the future.'

What does that mean?

'Anyway,' continues Medwick, 'you said a little bit of help would be appreciated, so here we are to offer some now! Do you think the Tharg that ran back to the zone saw you?'

'No,' I reply, 'definitely not.'

'In that case,' says Medwick, 'the guard at The Dark Castle zone should be minimal.

'I said that there might be a guard,' says Becky.

'Aah good,' says Medwick, 'so you already have a plan?'

He aims this question at me.

'No,' I reply, 'that's just what we had started to discuss when you arrived!'

'Oh, at least we're in time to give you our little piece of help! Herf, would you kindly do the honours?'

'Certainly, Medwick,' says Herf as he shuffles into position, 'but may I just correct Master Eddie on something before I begin?'

'What's that?' replies Medwick.

'Master Eddie called the monkeys "snow monkeys",' continues Herf, 'I feel that he should know their real name, in case he comes across them again.'

'Indeed,' says Medwick, 'go ahead.'

'Their real name, Master Eddie, is Rainbeye Monkeys because of their rainbow eyes.'

'Ok,' I say, 'thanks for that Herf.'

'And even though they prefer their snow, they can go elsewhere if necessary!'

'Thank you, Herf,' butts in Medwick, 'that's enough of that! Now explain to young Eddie how to get past the guard.' Herf shrinks back slightly before drawing breath and starting again.

'The guards need scaring away from the other zone before you transport,' says Herf, 'so…'

'So,' joins in Carrot, 'we send an Ayck through first!'

Herf and Medwick look at Carrot in amazement. In fact, we all look at Carrot in amazement.

'I didn't think you had a plan yet?' asks Medwick.

'We didn't!' I reply.

'I just thought of it!' exclaims Carrot.

'Well then,' says Medwick, 'congratulations are in order.'

'Yeah, well done,' we all say.

'But how do you suggest getting a 50lb swan to go onto the zone?' says Herf stubbornly.

'Entice it somehow?' suggests Liz.

'Yes, ok,' says an even more stubborn Herf, 'but what with!?'

I look at the others. We seem to have run out of suggestions.

'You have done extremely well,' says Medwick with what sounds like genuine praise in his voice, 'but finally, Herf, I think we can help our friends!'

'Good,' says Herf. 'The Aycks love the fruit of the remorc tree. There are several remorc trees around the lake, but the Aycks necks, however long they are, can only reach up so high; so, if you climb up to the higher branches and collect some fruit, placing that on the zone should be enough to get the Aycks to transport.'

'And when they see the guard at the other end, they should make the noise and scare them away?' I ask.

'Yes,' replies Herf.

'Isn't that unfair on the Ayck?' asks Becky. 'Sending it away from its family?'

'Once you have all safely transported,' explains Medwick, 'you can place some more fruit on the zone to allow the Ayck to return.'

'Ok,' I say, 'thank you, Medwick. Thank you, Herf. Any more advice?'

'I'm afraid that's it. Except to say that even though we're not a violent or particularly physical race, we do have the Palace guards who will assist you if necessary.'

'Thank you,' I say, 'that's good to know, but how do I get hold of them?'

'That would have been tricky, but now that the leaves are walking…'

'The leaves are walking…' echoes Herf.

'Anyway, all the best!' and Medwick turns to leave.

'Hang on,' I call after him, 'you can't just go like that!'

'We must,' replies Herf. 'If a Gingoile spends too long in the vicinity of the zone leading to The Dark Castle we may be discovered!'

'How?' asks Liz.

'Scent,' calls back Medwick who is moving away at quite a pace, closely followed by Herf.

'But won't they smell us?' I shout.

117

'No,' replies Medwick, 'your scent is too new at the moment. But the smell of us Gingoiles gets right up their noses!' And with that he steps onto the zone and disappears. Herf turns, waves and follows him!

# Chapter Twelve

'Ok,' I call up to Brian, 'that's a dozen. That will do.'

Brian climbs down from the remorc tree to join us.

'Shall we put six on now and take six with us?' asks Liz.

'Sounds fine to me,' I reply.

'Can I go and put them on the zone?' asks Becky.

'Sure,' I reply.

'I'll help,' says Carrot picking three remorc fruit up.

'Ok,' says Becky, 'let's go.'

They make their way around the back of the trees to the far side of the zone and place the fruit on it. Why the fruit doesn't transport I don't know. Medwick didn't explain. Maybe it's not heavy enough or not alive enough! Maybe I'll ask Medwick the next time I see him. Who knows when that will be!

One Ayck immediately spots the fruit and heads towards the zone. Becky and Carrot move back to a nearby tree where we join up with them.

'Right,' I say, 'when it goes, we'll give it 30 seconds then you follow, Brian. Ok?'

'Fine,' replies Brian.

'If there are any Thargs around,' I continue, 'return straight away. If the coast is clear hide in a tree or bush or wherever you can near to the zone. We'll come through as quick as we can.'

'Fine,' says Brian once more.

'It's going onto the zone,' says Liz. We all watch as the Ayck eats the third fruit it managed to reach with its long neck without stepping onto the zone before it finally is forced to step onto the zone to reach the remaining fruit.

'It's gone,' I say. 'Start the watch Carrot.'

'I'm on to it,' says Carrot.

It goes quiet as we watch Carrot watching his watch.

'Ok, Brian,' announces Carrot, 'time's up!'

'Ok,' says Brian. 'Here I go!'

'Good luck!' we all say almost in unison.

Now we all seem to just exchange furtive glances.

'Thirty seconds,' says Carrot. 'It must be clear.'

Or he's been caught, I think. But I daren't say it out loud.

'I'll go next,' says Liz.

'Take care, Sis,' I say.

She smiles at me as she steps onto the zone and disappears. Please be ok, please be ok, I keep repeating to myself.

'Your turn now, Eddie,' says Carrot.

'Ok, mate,' I reply, 'see you in a minute.'

I smile at both Carrot and Becky as I step onto the zone.

\*

Rocks and clouds. That's all I can see. Rocks on the ground and clouds, mostly dark grey clouds, in the sky. I look around and see Brian and Liz squatting behind a nearby rock. Oh, I forgot to mention, about ten feet away the Ayck is making its rather unique sound towards where I assume the Tharg guard once was.

'Ok?' I ask Brian and Liz as I join them behind the rock.

'Fine,' says Liz. 'Brian thinks he saw the back of a couple of Thargs going round that rockface down there.'

I follow her finger. It makes sense. That's the direction the Ayck is facing. It looks like Carrot was right to send the Ayck through first!

'Did they see you, Brian?' I ask.

'No,' replies Brian, 'they didn't turn around.'

'Alright?' asks Becky as she joins us.

'Yes,' I reply, 'let's wait for Carrot and we'll decide what to do next.'

'Here he is!' says Liz.

'Ok, mate?' I ask.

'Yes,' replies Carrot, 'bit grim round here, isn't it?'

'I wonder if it was always like this, or whether the fact that the Thargs live here and are in control has made it like this?' says Becky.

120

'I'll add that to my list of questions I have for Medwick!' I say.

'What now, mate?' asks Carrot.

'Well,' I say, 'Brian saw two Thargs disappear in that direction,' I point, 'so I think we should head in that direction,' I point between some other rocks, 'and try and get to some higher ground so that we can see The Dark Castle. How does that sound?'

'Fine to me, Bro'

'And me,' add Carrot and Brian.

'Can we let the poor Ayck go home now?' asks Becky.

'Of course,' I say, 'go ahead.' She creeps back to the zone and places the remaining six remorc fruit onto the zone. The Ayck is immediately aware of the fruit. Maybe it smells. It doesn't to me. It turns and makes its way onto the zone. Peace at last!

'Ok,' I say, 'we better go before the guards return. Will you lead please, Brian?'

'No problem,' he replies.

'Just take it steady and keep the noise down.'

Brian nods and leads us down a narrowish rocky path. I'm immediately looking around for a way to reach higher ground. For all I know we could be heading in completely the wrong direction, but we need to go up so we can see over all the cliffs and rocks that surround us. As we are walking, I start to feel a warmth coming from my pocket. The box! It hasn't given off warmth for ages.

'Hang on, everyone,' I say in a loud whisper, 'come over here.' I crouch behind a rock. The others join me.

'My box is glowing,' I say. 'I need to take a look at it.' I retrieve the box from my pocket and see that the lid is glowing. I slide the lid back and remove the map. I had put it back in the box for safe keeping once we'd discovered that all we needed to do was follow the zones engraved around the sides of the box. The map itself was quite simple.

I open the map.

'Amazing,' says Liz in astonishment.

'Wow,' say the others.

I'm speechless. The map has changed. No longer is it a very simple map, which was ultimately not a lot of use, but a very clear and very precise, at least I hope it is, map of the immediate area. I spread the map out.

'I think we're here,' says Carrot pointing to a narrow path leading away from the clearly marked zone.

'I agree,' I say.

'So, if we carry on down here,' adds Liz pointing on the map, 'we should be able to see The Dark Castle without climbing up on to higher ground.'

'It looks that way,' I say.

'What's the scale?' asks Carrot.

'One mile to ten inches,' I read from the bottom corner.

'Then we're not much more than half a mile away,' replies Carrot. 'Once we get out of this gorge, I think it will be quite obvious where The Dark Castle is with or without the map!'

I can feel the hairs rising on the back of my neck at the thought of only being half a mile away from The Dark Castle.

'Come on, then,' says Brian who seems eager to keep going to keep away from the two guards, whilst forgetting that he's leading us towards a castle full of Thargs!

'Ok,' I say as I slip the map into my pocket so it's a bit closer to hand rather than back in the box. 'Let's get to the end of this gorge and have a look at this castle.'

How did that map change? Why am I thinking that? It's no stranger than anything else that's currently happening. For starters I AM IN ANOTHER WORLD!!! So, a changing map is nothing!

Brian stops ahead of us so we all catch up.

'It looks like the end of the gorge,' says Brian.

'Ok,' I say getting onto my hands and knees, 'let's crawl round the corner and take a look!'

I take the lead and crawl round the last rock virtually on my belly. And there it is. A truly magnificent building. But for every beautiful white part of The Palace of The Realm, The Dark Castle is equally dark and menacing. The Castle is in a diamond shape. The South Tower is, as Medwick said it would be, at the front in the centre with a large door in it. Walls lead back from this tower at angles to the East and West Towers. Further walls lead back to the North Tower which is in alignment with the South Tower, but it is much higher. In fact, the whole castle seems to be higher the further away it goes. To top it all, the whole castle from the East and West Towers backwards is surrounded and overlooked by a vast mountain. I think the door in the South Tower is the only way in!

'It looks like the door in the South Tower is the only way in, Eddie,' says Carrot.

See!

'And that doesn't look too inviting!' adds Liz.

'I noticed,' I say. 'I need you all to study what you can see very hard and give me some ideas on how to get in there! It goes silent. I'm not surprised!

I look at the menacing view. One heavily fortified castle with only one way in. That entrance is not only a closed, heavy looking door, but a door which is looked down upon by Thargs walking around the battlements at the top of the walls. How to get in!!!???

'It might be easier at night,' offers Becky. 'You know, in the dark.'

'They would still need to leave the door unlocked and unguarded!' replies Carrot with a smile.

It goes quiet again.

'We need some sort of distraction,' says Liz. 'Something over the cliffs to make them think they're being attacked from the rear, or at least to make them turn around!'

'That sounds a reasonable idea,' I say, 'but even if we could think of a distraction we'd still, as Carrot said, need them to leave the door unlocked!'

'Maybe we should sleep on it,' says Carrot, 'it's getting a bit dark.'

'And at least we can study the castle overnight,' adds Liz, 'so that we can see how many guards they have and how well lit up it is.'

'Ok,' I reply. 'Where shall we camp?'

'There's a cave over there' says Brian pointing behind us, 'we can take turns on lookout and be able to see the path to the zone and the castle from the entrance way.'

We all look astonished at Brian, our King of the Senses, once more. We're all discussing things and I'm thinking that Brian has nothing to add, yet here he is with a planned-out night for us all!

'Brilliant, Brian,' I say, 'great job. Let's go and take a look!'

I crawl away on my belly towards the cave.

*

It's ok in here. The cave. Carrot made a fire with two sticks. We all told him it wouldn't work, but it did, eventually. Liz was worried the light would be seen from the outside, but the cave is deep and sort of curved so I think we're ok. We've been taking it in turns to keep lookout. I say "we" but the others won't let me take a turn with me being next in line to the throne and all that! Brian's at the edge of the cave now keeping an eye out. The rest of us are sleeping. Well, I'm obviously not sleeping at the moment, but I was! Something woke me up. Some sort of noise. I don't know what it was and it doesn't seem to have disturbed the others or sent Brian rushing in, so I guess it's nothing.

I'm thinking that a distraction of the Tharg guards is possible, but I still can't think of how to get through that huge door. More sleep is needed.

*

'Eddie, Eddie! Come and look!' It's Liz who's shaking me quite firmly.

'What is it?' I slur.

'Just come' she says dragging me up.

Brian and Becky are huddled around Becky's knapsack. I guess Carrot is on lookout.

'The Ayck egg is hatching, Eddie!' enthuses Liz.

And there it is, being watched by a bemused Brian and a beaming Becky.

'I thought I heard a noise earlier in the night,' I say. 'Maybe it was the egg?'

'Maybe,' replies Becky. 'I was woken up a few times earlier in the night by a noise.'

We all quieten down and watch as a swan's beak, or is it bill, starts to force its way through the shell. It's not long before a head is peeping through. Much to my surprise, unlike a swan which doesn't look much like a swan when it's young, the Ayck appears to be just like an adult in colour, but smaller.

'Come on,' pleads Becky, 'you can do it!' The Ayck seems to have spotted the direction of the first words it hears and turns its head towards Becky.

'It now thinks you're its mum!' says Liz.

'So it should,' joins Brian, 'you have been looking after it!'

Becky smiles, 'nearly there, little one!'

There is a strange noise.

'What was that?' asks Liz.

'I don't know,' I reply.

The noise happens again.

'I think it's the Ayck,' suggests Brian.

Then I hear the noise again. It is. The Ayck is making some sort of throaty noise.

'Oh, that's sweet,' says Becky.

'Yes,' adds Liz.

It does it again.

'But it's getting louder,' I say. 'Can you stop it?!'

'How can I stop it?' says Becky.

'I was just wondering if it thinks you're its mother then it may only take instruction from you!'

'What do you want her to say to it?' asks Liz. 'Please quieten down, we're hiding from the Thargs!'

'I don't know,' I say, 'but something needs to happen otherwise we won't be hiding from the Thargs much longer!'

'What's that noise?'

It's Carrot who has obviously heard the noise from the cave entrance.

'The Ayck's born!' states Brian.

'And Eddie expects me to be able to turn the volume down on it,' adds Becky.

I just look at Carrot. No point saying anything at the moment. Not only would it probably not be appreciated, but I would have to time my talking in between the increasingly louder Ayck outbursts!

'Maybe you could make the same noises back to the Ayck, but quieter,' suggests Carrot. 'Then it might copy you!'

What a good idea!

'Do you think it might work?' asks Liz.

'Worth a shot,' replies Carrot. 'We need to do something otherwise Thargs are going to start hearing the noises echoing over their castle.'

'Try it, Becky,' says Liz.

'Ok, but no laughing!'

We all give Becky room. She starts by taking the last few pieces of shell off the Ayck's back and picking it up and putting it on her lap. This seems to take the edge off the volume.

'Try making the noise softly now,' suggests Carrot.

Becky nods. She then starts mimicking the Ayck, but in very hushed tones. Quite quickly the Ayck follows Becky's lead and quietens down.

'Well done,' says a beaming Brian.

'Brilliant idea, Carrot,' adds Liz.

'Anyone got any remorc fruit for it?' I ask.

'I put some in my bag,' replies Becky.

'I'll get it,' says Liz. The much quieter bird watches Liz retrieve the fruit. It can obviously smell it even before it appears, and gently takes it from Liz's hand.

'I'll get back on watch,' says Carrot.

'Well done, mate,' I say as Carrot moves towards the cave entrance and away from the bizarre scene of a swan-like creature being hand-fed fruit!

Liz and Brian stay near to Becky who is now cooing quietly as the Ayck is eating the remorc. I decide to settle back down and try and get more sl......

'Eddie, Eddie!' It's Carrot who's shouting in a loud whisper at me from across the cave.

'What's up?' I reply.

'Quick! Come and look at this.' He beckons me towards the cave entrance.

'What is it?' I ask as I get up.

'It's unbelievable. Quick.' He disappears around the curve in the cave. I look at the others.

'Want us to come?' asks Liz.

'No idea,' I reply. 'I'm guessing it's nothing bad seeing as he went back out again!'

'I'll come with you,' says Brian.

'Ok!'

I have no idea what Carrot has seen. How can it be unbelievable? Everything here is unbelievable!

'Stop, Eddie,' whispers Carrot as I reach the mouth of the cave. 'Look!'

I look and see nothing.

'What am I looking for?' I ask.

'Over there, on the ground. Stand here, you can see it better in the moonlight from here.'

I look and still see nothing.

'Oh yes,' says Brian, 'I can see it!'

'See what!' I say. Before I finish the 't' of 'what' Brian has got hold of me and positioned me so I can't fail to see it. Words. On the floor. Written in leaves.

'"Need help?"' I say. 'Is that what it says? "Need help?"'

'Looks like it,' says Brian.

'Yes, it does,' exclaims Carrot excitedly. 'I came in when I heard the Ayck noise and when I came back out here, there it was; "Need help?"'

'Who wrote it?' I ask, 'someone has come up here and laid leaves out to contact us, but who?'

'No one,' replies Carrot, 'at least I don't think so.'

'Sorry Carrot, you've lost me,' I say.

'"The leaves are walking" that's what Medwick said didn't he? "The leaves are walking."'

'Oh yes,' adds Brian, 'the arrows from the leaves before.'

'Of course,' I say, 'I'm tired, I forgot about that!'

I'm not really that tired, I just forgot!

'So; what now?' asks Carrot.

'Maybe we just say yes!' replies Brian.

'Yes, to who?' asks Carrot.

'To the leaves,' continues Brian. 'They're asking if we want help. I think we do!'

You're not wrong there, Brian.

'So, shall I just say yes, to the leaves?' I ask.

'Worth a shot,' replies Carrot.

Ok. So, it's the middle of the night, in another world and on top of everything else I am now about to start talking to leaves!

'If you're offering us help,' I say whilst looking down roughly towards the 'd' in "Need help?", 'the answer is yes… please!'

I pause and look at the other two, who are exchanging glances with me, each other and the leaves. There's no movement. I'm now thinking that someone may have laid the leaves on the ground.

'Look,' says Brian trying to stay calm, 'they're moving.'

He's right! The leaves are gently blowing around even though there is no wind. They're sort of getting upright and even though they don't have any legs they do look like they're walking. The leaves are walking!

'"OK,"' says Brian. 'They're writing "OK."' He's right. The leaves are somehow communicating with each other and forming the letters "OK".

'Now what?' asks Carrot.

I shrug towards Carrot and turn back to the leaves.

'Thanks,' I say towards the leaves, 'do you have any idea how to get into the Castle?'

Brian and Carrot look at me as if I'm stupid! I just think I might as well get any help I can.

'They're moving again,' says Brian.

They shift around in a beautiful, entrancing way.

'"Make noise",' reads Carrot. 'What do they mean by that?'

The leaves do now spell out "make noise".

'That's the last thing we want to do, isn't it?' continues Carrot.

The leaves are now moving again.

'"Behind castle",' I read as the leaves settle down once more.

'"Make noise behind castle",' I say to the leaves 'Why? How?'

I look up at the huge castle dimly lit by moonlight with the towering cliffs behind it. Not possible! The leaves are walking again.

'"Use Ayck",' reads Carrot.

What? They start to walk again.

'"One hour",' continues Carrot.

'"Use Ayck, one hour"!' I exclaim. 'What on earth does that mean?'

As I speak, the leaves just fly away as if caught by a gust of wind, but there is still no wind.

'Any thoughts?' I ask.

Brian just shrugs.

'I'm guessing,' offers Carrot, 'that in one hour's time the leaves want the Ayck to make a noise behind the castle to cause a distraction.'

Sounds reasonable.

'Then what?' asks Brian.

'Then,' I say, 'I'm guessing they'll help us get in whilst the Thargs are distracted.'

'How?' asks Carrot.

'I don't know,' I reply. 'If the leaves had hung around a bit longer, I would have asked them!'

'I think we should go back into the cave,' suggests Brian, sensibly.

'Quite right,' I reply.

Brian leads us back into the cave. Should we really be listening to a bunch of leaves?

The cave is nice and quiet. The Ayck is asleep on Becky's lap.

'What was out there?' inquires Liz.

129

'A message from the leaves,' replies Carrot in a manner that makes it sound normal to be having a conversation with a bunch of leaves!

'You what!?' is Liz's startled reply.

'It's true,' I say, 'not only, as Medwick and Herf said, are the leaves walking; they're also communicating!'

'What was the message?' asks Becky in a hushed voice as she cradles the sleeping Ayck.

'"Make noise behind castle",' joins Brian.

'What does that mean?' asks Liz.

'We think they want us to distract the Thargs before helping us get in,' I reply.

'How?' asks Becky.

'With him,' says Carrot pointing at the Ayck.

'What?' replies Becky.

'The leaves wrote "use Ayck, one hour",' I say.

'How can he distract them?' asks Liz.

'Dunno,' I say.

'Well,' says Carrot. 'Thargs don't like Aycks, do they?'

'No,' replies Becky who's continuing to cuddle the Ayck, 'but they run from big Aycks. Alan's only a baby Ayck.' Alan? Who's Alan?

'Who's Alan?' asks Brian.

See!

'Everybody,' announces Becky whilst nodding down towards the Ayck, 'this is Alan the Ayck!'

'Why Alan?' asks Carrot.

'It just seemed to go!' replies Becky.

'It's the noise,' blurts out Brian.

'I beg your pardon, Brian,' I say.

'The Thargs don't run from the Aycks because of their size,' continues Brian, 'they run from the noise they make!'

'You're right!' I exclaim, 'if the Ayck... sorry... Alan can fly to the rear of the castle and make a noise, he may distract them!'

Everyone stares at me. What have I said? It seems to me that's exactly what the leaves want us to do. How else can we use the Ayck?

'Sounds fair enough to me!' says Carrot, eventually.

Thank you, mate.

'Sounds fair enough!' says Becky in what can no longer be referred to as hushed tones. 'How can sending a newly hatched bird over the heads of dangerous Thargs be fair enough? And,' she continues without pausing for breath, 'how do I tell it to make a noise once at the rear of the castle?'

I think she may have us there!

'You taught it to quieten down,' says Liz.

Becky stares at Liz.

'So, you're on their side too?'

'No,' replies Liz, 'I'm just thinking that the leaves must think it's possible and when you made the quieter noise, Alan copied you.'

We look at Becky cuddling the Ayck as if it's her long-lost favourite doll.

'It might work, but I don't want to see him get hurt,' says Becky.

'They just seem to run from them, Becky,' says Carrot, 'they don't seem to attack them.'

'Those were just guards running away,' replies Becky, 'they might have weapons that they use against them at the castle.'

'I'm afraid that's a risk we're going to have to take,' says Liz whilst putting an arm around Becky's shoulder. 'Uncle Mark and all the Gingoiles are relying on us.'

It goes quiet. We all find ourselves sitting down, waiting for Becky's reply.

'Even if I say yes,' starts Becky, 'and even if I can make Alan make a loud noise; how am I going to get him to fly to the rear of the castle? He'll just make the noise here and attract the Thargs.... All of them!'

Eyes are upon me once more.

'Food,' I say, 'they seem to make the most noise when they're hungry.'

'But the food is here, Bro, not behind the castle!'

'How about this,' says Carrot producing a small catapult from one of his umpteen hidden pockets.

'Why on earth have you got that?' asks Liz.

'Well,' answers Carrot, 'you never know!'

'It's very small,' says Becky.

'But it's designed to go a long way.'

'How far have you managed?' I venture.

'I've easily cleared the length of the school playing field.'

'That won't be far enough,' says Liz.

'No,' says Carrot, 'but I reckon Brian could make it go further.'

'What do you reckon, Brian,' I ask.

'Hang on,' says Brian as he dashes out of the cave.

'Where's he going?' asks Becky.

'No idea,' I reply 'Gather all the remorc fruit we have. Whatever happens, we're gonna need it.'

'Not from here,' says Brian reappearing at the cave opening, 'but there are some trees much nearer the castle wall which I should be able to get to in the dark and use the catapult from there.'

'Do you think you'll be able to reach the back of the castle from there?' asks Carrot.

'I'll try,' replies Brian. 'I reckon it's a good three times the length of the school playing field though.'

Eyes upon the next in line again. That's me!

'Well,' I announce, 'unless anyone has any other kind of plan, we'll have to give it a try.'

'And we've got 40 minutes to get it sorted,' says Carrot, peering at his watch in the golden glow of our cave fire.

## Chapter Thirteen

I really can't see this working. Brian and Carrot have made their way down to some trees nearer to the wall of The Dark Castle. They didn't seem to have any difficulty getting there. The Thargs have some guards wandering along the top of the castle wall, but no search lights or anything else. I guess they don't know we're in The Realm yet, otherwise there would probably be more guards and lights! I suppose that after a hundred years they're maybe not concentrating on guarding as much as they should be? Well, I'm hoping they're not! Carrot's gone with Brian so he can explain exactly how his catapult works! I'm sure Brian's used one before! He's also the one with the best watch, so he says, so he can tell Brian exactly when the leaves want him to start the distraction.

'What do you think the leaves are going to do once Alan causes the distraction?' asks Liz.

'I've been pondering that one for ages, Sis,' I reply. 'I really don't know. What can a bunch of leaves do?'

'They are walking leaves, Eddie, remember that!' says Liz.

'I can't imagine what any kind of leaves can do against a huge castle wall!'

'Alan's asleep!' says Becky walking towards us from the cave entrance.

'Asleep!' I say. 'He's supposed to be flying over that castle in less than five minutes!'

'I know,' replies Becky calmly, 'I thought I'd wake him up and tempt him with some of the remorc fruit in the cave and try and get him to make the noise.'

'Won't that attract the attention of the Thargs?' asks Liz.

'Maybe,' replies Becky, 'but hopefully they'll soon be distracted away from the cave as he flies over their heads!'

'Flies!' I exclaim.

'Yes,' says Becky, 'what about it?'

'We don't even know if he can fly.' Becky looks at me with a rather worried expression on her face. I nod in agreement.

'I'd already thought of that,' says Liz, 'but I assume the leaves wouldn't have suggested it if they didn't think Alan could fly.'

True.

'We'll soon find out,' I say. 'I make it two minutes to go!'

'Shall I wake him now?' asks Becky.

'I don't know,' I reply, 'I'm waiting for some sort of sign.'

'Something like that?' says Liz pointing out towards the open space in front of the castle.

'I guess that's as good a sign as any,' I say as I watch hundreds, or even thousands, of leaves silently wafting across the ground towards the wall.

'I'll get Alan,' says Becky as she heads back into the cave.

'What do we do?' asks Liz.

'I suppose we run towards the leaves once the guards are distracted?' I offer.

'What; straight across the open ground?' asks Liz.

'It's probably better if we skirt round the edge towards Carrot and Brian,' I reply, 'just in case one of the guards isn't completely distracted.'

'Right, there's the sign from Carrot,' I say as I see a torchlight flashing. 'Guess they've seen the leaves and Brian is ready with the catapult... What's that noise?'

We both turn towards the cave as Becky comes out of it, holding Alan and making the same ridiculous noise as him.

'That's too loud!' says Liz, but I don't think Becky can hear her.

'Look,' I say in the quietest shout I can muster, 'Brian's launching the fruit... let Alan go!' I make a huge gesture towards Becky who, thankfully, gets the gist and throws the Ayck skywards. We all stand staring at this bizarre swan-like creature who is just circling above our heads.

'What now?' shouts Becky above the din.

As she says this a huge bright spotlight picks up Alan above our heads.

'Hit the deck,' I shout as I dive to the ground hoping we haven't been spotted. Liz and Becky follow suit.

'Make him follow the fruit,' shouts Liz towards Becky.

'How do I do that?' is the reply.

'Hang on!' I say as I see Alan change direction and head towards the castle, 'I think he's spotted the fruit!'

We all look up as Alan, still making a racket, starts to head towards the castle with the spotlight trying to keep up with him.

'Quick,' I say, 'follow me!'

I get up and start running from tree to tree around the edge of the open space towards Carrot and Brian. Liz and Becky are close behind. I can see Brian continuously firing remorc fruit over the walls of The Dark Castle. I wouldn't say he's firing them completely to the back of the castle, but they're going a long way. As we reach Carrot and Brian, the Ayck has cleared the walls and the spotlight is now pointing towards the back of the castle. We can hear the melee going on inside the castle as Alan makes his endless noise.

'Well done you two,' I offer as I approach Carrot and Brian.

'What now?' asks Carrot, whilst handing another piece of fruit to Brian for him to fire.

'Look!' exclaims Liz.

We all turn to stare at the leaves which are wafting around near the base of the huge outer wall. Out of the pile of leaves a column starts to rise; a column of leaves that is.

'What are they doing?' asks Becky.

No one replies, we just watch. The column reaches the top of the wall then, staying against the wall, steps start to come out of the column towards us.

'Steps!' I say, just in case the others hadn't worked out what they were! 'They want us to climb the steps to get over the wall!'

'Steps made of leaves,' says Liz. 'How on earth are they going to hold our weight?'

'Well, they are magic leaves,' I say.

'Whatever we're going to do,' says Carrot, 'we need to do it now because we've run out of fruit!'

'I'll go,' says Brian, 'if they can hold me they can hold any of us!'

I need to make a quick decision.

'Ok, Brian, go for it!'

Brian hands the catapult to Carrot and runs to the leaves. As he starts to climb the leaves, they seem to give a bit, like a sponge, but they hold him. Brian turns and waves to the rest of us to follow. I nod towards Becky who runs over to the steps and starts to follow Brian up the leaves.

'Your turn now Bro,' says Liz.

'Ok,' I say as I head off towards the leaf stairway. As I step on the leaves, they do give a little but then I can almost feel each individual leaf pushing me back up through the sole of my shoe. I look ahead of me, up the stairs, just as Becky hops over the top of the wall and out of sight.

'This way,' calls out Brian as I stick my head over the wall. Both he and Becky are leaning against the inside of the wall on a reasonably wide ledge which appears to run, just like battlements, around the inside of the outer wall.

'You both ok?' I ask.

'Yes,' they both reply, 'but I'm worried about Alan,' adds Becky.

I look up and see Alan circling the open central area of the castle with several bits of remorc fruit clumsily lodged between his legs and feet. As I watch, javelin-like weapons appear in the spotlight which is trying to keep up with Alan.

'What are they?' I ask.

'Those Thargs down there,' says Brian pointing, 'are trying to hit Alan. But they're not a very good shot. They've thrown loads and are getting nowhere near him.' Liz and Carrot have now joined us.

'Poor Alan,' says Liz.

'Don't worry,' I say, 'Brian's been watching them and says they're useless shots.'

'But they might get lucky,' says Liz. 'Can't we get the leaves to do something?'

'They all wafted away as soon as I reached the top of the wall,' replies Carrot. 'They've disappeared!'

We all look down at the Thargs who are throwing the weapons.

'What have they got on their ears?' asks Becky.

We look closer. Some strange black things appear to be over the ears of the Thargs.

'What do you make of it, Brian?' I ask.

'I've already noticed them,' replies our King of Senses, 'they look like some sort of headphones.'

'Why would they be wearing headphones?' asks Carrot.

'To block out the noise of the Aycks,' replies Liz.

'Yes,' I say, 'the only Thargs we can see are wearing the headphones. That must be their protective clothing when dealing with Aycks!'

'There were more Thargs around when I first got to the top of the wall,' says Brian, 'but they all disappeared and then the ones with the headphones on turned up.'

'Well spotted,' I say. 'If we could get rid of their headphones then maybe the Aycks could be more useful in the future.'

'Maybe,' says Becky, 'but what about Alan?'

'He's got to want to stop and eat all the fruit he's holding at some point,' says Liz.

'I'm afraid we can't sit around and wait,' I say, 'we need to get off this ledge before any guards return.'

'We can't leave him,' says Becky.

'Looks like he's having far too much fun dodging those spears!' says Carrot.

'I'm sure he'll leave and eat the fruit once he's had enough!' I offer. 'Is there a way down, Brian?'

'Yes,' he replies, 'just along the wall are some steps down into the castle.'

'Lead on.'

We all crawl along the ledge behind Brian. Becky does not look happy about leaving Alan. But we need to prioritise.

'Down here,' whispers Brian.

We all follow him down some rough stone stairs which open out into a long passageway with rooms coming off it.

'Thargs!' whispers Brian. 'In here!'

We all scurry into a room which Brian has entered.

'Ssh,' says Carrot as he closes the door behind us, 'I think there are three or four Thargs coming along the passageway.'

'Hide,' I say, 'in case they come in here.'

We all look around. There's not a lot to hide in or behind. I see Carrot crawl behind an old trunk. Brian ducks behind a sort of chest of drawers thing in the corner and the girls squeeze into a dodgy looking wardrobe. I can hear the footsteps getting louder. I make my mind up and follow Carrot behind the trunk.

'Budge up, mate,' I whisper to Carrot.

'It's a bit tight!' is his squashed reply.

Click.

'What's that?' asks Carrot.

Click.

'Ssh!' I say, 'I think those Thargs are coming in!'

I take a deep breath and watch Carrot's face drain of any colour it had.

'Injat spoilk Ayck,' I can hear one Tharg say.

'Panjoil dak skark,' comes the voice of another Tharg.

I'm still holding my breath. I can now hear the sound of a drawer opening. Are they by the chest of drawers near Brian? Please stay still, Brian.

Thud. Is that the drawer closing? I can't see anything except Carrot's face which is continuing to turn whiter and whiter.

'Darak Ayck hinklim.'

Click.

Was that the door again? I'm not sure I want to look in case it's a trick and they're still inside the room.

'It's ok,' says Brian, 'they've gone.'

I drag myself out from behind the trunk followed by Carrot. The girls poke their heads out of the cupboard door.

'How did you know they'd gone and not just closed the door behind them?' I ask.

'The damp smell disappeared!' replies Brian.

'I never noticed any smell,' says Liz, 'did anyone else?'

'No,' is the reply from Becky and Carrot.

'Nor me,' I say, 'well done, again, Brian!'

Brian beams.

'What were they doing in here?' asks Becky. 'I heard them say the word Ayck a couple of times.'

138

'So did I,' says Carrot, whose colour is slowly returning to his cheeks.

'I hope they didn't get him,' says Becky glumly.

'They didn't sound particularly happy,' I offer. 'More relieved.'

'Maybe,' replies Becky.

'Did they go in one of the drawers near you?' I ask Brian.

'Yes,' he replies, 'I can't believe they didn't see me!'

'Obviously their eyesight isn't as good as yours!' says Liz.

We all chuckle.

'Let's have a look,' I say. 'Which drawer was it, Brian?'

'The top one.'

I go to open the drawer.

'Careful Bro, it could be booby-trapped!' says Liz pulling me back. 'I'll do it.'

'It's just a drawer!' I say.

'Even so, we need to be careful all the time. Medwick did say something about things not always being what they seem.'

'Ok,' I reply.

No point arguing over opening a drawer now, is there!?

'Headphones,' says Liz as she opens the drawer. 'They've put those funny headphones in here.'

I reach in and take some out.

'Shall we break them?' asks Brian.

'Hang on,' I reply, 'what's this little switch here?' I flick a switch on one of the earpieces and loud heavy metal music starts to explode from the headphones. I look up at the others as I quickly flick the switch off again.

'So,' says Liz, 'the headphones don't just blank out the noise of the Aycks, they actually play music to them so as to completely block out the screeching Aycks!'

'That's if you can call that music,' says Carrot.

'I guess it has to be loud enough to drown out the noise of the Aycks,' says Liz.

'I think I prefer the Aycks over that!' replies Carrot.

We all smile.

'Clever,' I say, 'and I think we can be a bit more subtle than just breaking these, Brian. Do you have a screwdriver, Carrot?'

Carrot starts his coat-patting dance again.

'Yes, I do,' is the unsurprising answer. 'Here it is,' he says as he produces a miniature set of screwdrivers from another, as yet, unnamed pocket!

'I use these to open up my watch and those annoying little battery compartments on toys. Will they do?'

I hand Carrot a set of headphones. 'Do you think you could open up this annoying little compartment on these headphones?' I ask.

Carrot takes the headphones and starts to unscrew the tiny screw which is holding the earpiece together.

'Now what?' says Carrot as he hands the headphones back to me.

'Now,' I say, 'we flick this little wire and hopefully the sound is disconnected.' I hand the headphones back to Carrot. 'Screw the cover back on and try the switch,' I say.

We all wait as Carrot does this.

'Here goes,' says Carrot as he turns the switch on.

Nothing! It's worked!

'Well done, Eddie,' says Becky.

'Thanks,' I reply, 'now let's do it to all the others!'

'That will take ages,' says Brian.

'No, it won't,' I say, 'not if we all do it. You've got enough little screwdrivers haven't you, Carrot?'

'Yep!'

'But it would be a lot quicker if we just smashed them all up,' says Brian.

'It would,' I say, 'but if the Thargs happen to look in the drawer and see smashed up headphones they'll immediately know something's up. Whereas, if the headphones look alright, they'll not worry and they'll only notice a problem if they wear them. We don't want to attract any undue attention, do we?'

That speech sounded good.

'That makes sense, Bro.'

'Thanks!'

'Ok,' says Brian, 'I understand. Pass me a screwdriver!'

*

Twenty headphones sorted. Twenty! We did the top drawer, which held the six pairs we heard the Tharg put back. Then Brian opened the next two drawers which had another fourteen pairs between them! Anyway, it didn't take us that long.

'What now?' asks Becky.

'Well,' I say, 'we came over the outer wall to the west of the South Tower, so if we carry on the same way we should end up at the West Tower.'

'And hopefully the formula will be there,' adds Carrot.

'If not?' asks Becky.

'Then we make our way to the East Tower,' I say.

'Past the North Tower, so we can try and rescue Uncle Mark?' says Liz.

'Or back this way,' says Carrot, 'which would probably be easier because we'd have already gone along some of the route before.'

Liz pulls a face at Carrot and looks like she's about to have a go at him.

'We'll decide what to do after we've been to the West Tower,' I say quite strongly. 'Ok?'

Both Liz and Carrot give me sheepish nods.

'Now,' I continue, 'all we need is a map. We can't go wandering around this huge castle hoping to just appear at the right place!'

'Then get the map out, Eddie,' says Liz.

Oh yeah, the map. I'd forgotten about that.

'But that's of the surrounding area,' says Carrot, 'not of The Dark Castle.'

'But it changed from our route to The Dark Castle to the surrounding area,' continues Liz, 'so it may change again!'

She's right.

'I'll take a look,' I say as I reach in to my pocket.

I slowly unfold the map and....

'Unbelievable,' says Becky, 'it has changed again!'

We all look once more at the map, with our mouths wide open. There it is. A precise plan of the whole of The Dark Castle.

'You're right Sis, it has changed again,' I manage to mutter.

'Why didn't Medwick tell us of this?' asks Carrot.

'There are lots of things he hasn't been telling us, isn't there?' I say as I look round my friends faces, 'but he did say things aren't always as they seem. Maybe he was referring to this map?'

'Maybe,' replies Carrot.

'What's that?' says Brian who has been peering over Carrot's head at the map.

'What?' I reply.

'That little red dot, there!' he says pointing to a tiny dot on one of the rooms on the map.

'I think that's where we are!' says Liz. We all look closely.

'You're right!' exclaims Carrot. 'We came in here,' he continues pointing, 'down this passageway and into this room!'

Carrot is now pointing at the dot.

'How can the map know where we are?' asks Becky.

'How can the map change itself?' replies Liz, whilst smiling at her best friend.

'Exactly,' I say, 'clearly anything is possible in The Realm and what we have here is some sort of satnavmap!'

The others look up from the map and give me unconvincing expressions.

'You know,' I press on, 'like a satnav in a car tracks a car, this map is sort of tracking us!'

'Sounds fair enough to me!' says Carrot.

Thanks, mate!

'Whatever it's called,' says Liz, 'let's work out a route to the West Tower.'

*

142

I don't like the feel of this. We studied the map and agreed a route, but it looked too simple. Along this corridor, down some steps, along another corridor, up some steps and bingo! The West Tower. Find the formula and retrace our steps....

'How are we going to get out again?' whispers Carrot. 'Once we've got the formula. The leaves have gone!'

I hadn't thought of that.

'One thing at a time, Carrot,' I reply.

'But there's no point in getting the formula if we can't get it to the Gingoiles, is there?' continues Carrot.

I glance across to Liz. Help Sis!

'Maybe the leaves are watching from the trees and will help us when we return to the wall,' offers Liz.

'And maybe Alan is watching from the cliff and will help to cause a distraction again,' ventures Becky.

I look at Carrot and shrug. 'You never know!'

Carrot doesn't look impressed with our thoughts.

'Patrol,' whispers Brian who's been leading us down our first corridor. 'In here!'

We all follow Brian into another room and dive behind various bits of furniture like we did in the last room. This time I'm behind a curtain with Brian.

'They've gone past,' says Brian after a minute or so.

'How do you know?' I ask.

'I heard their feet go past the door.'

How does he do it? I didn't hear a thing!

'Ok, it's clear,' I say as I grapple my way out from behind the curtain.

'We can't keep diving into any old room,' says Liz, 'there might be Thargs in any of them.

'I do listen at the door and have a good sniff as I open it,' replies Brian. 'I wouldn't have brought you in here if I thought there were any Thargs in here!'

We all exchange glances. You really can't knock Brian for his perception and observation!

'Do you want to check the map again?' asks Carrot. 'Just to check that it is a satnav thingy and that the red dot is now in this room?'

'Ok,' I say as I get the map out of my pocket and unfold it.

'Here we are,' says Carrot pointing to the red dot, 'in the right room. Looks like you're right Eddie!'

I smile. Nice to be right sometimes!

'What's this?' asks Brian pointing to a faint blue dot in the same room as us.

'No idea,' I say as I look around the room. 'There's nobody in here but us.'

'Maybe it's not showing a someone, but a something,' says Becky.

'I'm not sure I follow,' says Carrot.

Nor do I!

'Well,' continues Becky, 'it's blue and not red. Maybe red is human and blue is an object. And it's a faint blue, suggesting it's hidden out of view.'

'How about in here,' suggests Brian who has walked away from us and is standing by a large trunk. 'The blue dot seems to be coming from this end of the room.'

I look at the map again. 'I think you're right.'

'Shall I open it?' asks Brian.

'Guess so,' I reply.

'Be careful,' whispers Becky frantically.

Brian smiles at Becky and turns his attention to the trunk.

'Anything in there?' I ask Brian as the trunk creaks open.

'Just some blankets,' he replies. 'I'll take them out.'

'Look!' says Carrot, 'the blue dot on the map is definitely getting clearer.'

'You're right,' I say, 'keep taking those blankets out Brian. There's something at the bottom of the trunk.'

'Nothing at the bottom, Eddie,' says Brian, 'just this stone.'

Brian's holding a stone in his hand. More of a palm-sized smooth pebble rather than a stone.

'Let me see it Brian,' I ask.

'The blue dot on the map is really clear now,' says Carrot, 'so it must be the stone.'

'Anything else in the trunk at all, Brian?'

'Nothing, Eddie.'

Brian hands me the stone. Just a smooth, largish pebble. Something you might pick up from any beach.

'I can't believe this is the thing making the blue dot appear on the map,' I say, 'red dot for us, blue dot for a stone? It doesn't make sense. It's just a stone!'

'That's because it's not just a stone!'

'Who said that?' I say looking around at the others.

'None of us,' says Becky.

'What do you mean "None of us"?' I say.

'We didn't say anything Bro,' says Liz.

'Then who said "That's because it's not a stone"?' I continue.

'I did!' comes the voice again. We all look around the room.

'Ok,' says Carrot, 'I'm not liking this now.'

'It's the stone,' offers Brian.

'You what,' I say as I look down at the stone.

'The voice is coming from the stone,' repeats Brian.

'Well done, Brian, you worked it out,' comes the voice from the stone.

We all look at the stone. I somehow keep hold of it even though I have an urge to drop it and run away!

'Is that you, Medwick?' asks Liz whilst staring at the stone which is laying in the palm of my hand.

'Yes, it's me, Liz,' comes the voice which really does seem to be emanating from the big pebble.

'Erm,' I stutter, 'how comes you're in a stone?' I ask.

Silly question, really!

'I'm not in the stone, Master Eddie, I'm at home!' Told you it was a silly question! 'This is just my voice you're hearing. It's called a GCD. A bit like the telephones in your world.'

'What does GCD stand for?' asks Carrot.

'Gingoile Communication Device,' replies Medwick.

145

'Hang on,' says Becky, 'we asked Flounge about communication devices and he said he wouldn't say.'

'That's correct,' replies Medwick, 'and he didn't say. You worked out the transporters, but didn't work out the GCDs!'

'I haven't seen anything that looks like telephones anywhere we've been,' says Brian.

'That's because, like this stone, most of our GCDs look like anything but a normal communication device.'

'Why?' asks Becky.

I was thinking that!

'Well,' replies Medwick, 'the Thargs thought they would weaken us by removing our GCDs, so old Krunk started to design them as all different things instead. The Thargs think they've confiscated them all, but most of us Gingoiles either own or have access to one of Krunk's camouflaged GCDs.'

'I don't know why I'm bothering to ask this,' I say, 'but why didn't you tell us about the GCDs?'

'Well,' replies Medwick, 'as you say, I don't know why you're bothering to ask!'

'You just expected us to work it out ourselves as usual?' adds Carrot.

'Quite!' is Medwick's brief reply.

'So, why did this GCD show on the map?' I ask.

'Well,' replies Medwick, 'some of Krunk's earliest camouflaged GCDs went missing due to them being so well camouflaged, so he started to put trackers on them which would show up on the map. Clever, eh?'

'Until a Tharg gets a map,' says Carrot.

'Yes, but that's not going to happen is it, young Carrot?' rasps Medwick.

Carrot rolls his eyes at me.

'Can I ask why one of your communication devices is in The Dark Castle?' asks Liz.

Good question.

'Well,' says Medwick whilst making a coughing noise. I think he's clearing his throat. 'You see, erm, it was your uncle's.' There is silence as we all look down at the smooth pebble sitting in my hand.

'This was Uncle Mark's?' I finally say.

'Yes, Master Eddie. It was on his person when he was captured.'

'Did you know it was here?' asks Liz.

'Good gracious, no!' replies Medwick. 'We thought it had just been thrown away.'

'Then how did you know we had it when you started talking to us?' asks Liz.

'Well, this was one of Krunk's greatest GCDs,' replies Medwick. 'He designed it so that it would only work if a member of the Ross family touched it. As soon as Eddie started talking whilst holding it I could hear him through my GCD.'

Amazing!

'Very clever,' says Carrot.

'Thank you, young Carrot,' says Medwick.

'Just one thing,' continues Carrot, 'why a stone? Surely a pencil or watch would have been better for Mark to have carried around with him.'

'True,' comes the voice from the stone, 'but Krunk couldn't get the technology to work any smaller than this. Anyway, I guess the Thargs would have taken everything off of the Ruler when they captured him, whatever it looked like!'

'Why didn't you give us a GCD when we first left you?' asks Becky.

'Because, Becky, you would have relied on it too much. You would have contacted me with "how do we get along the waterfall edge; how do we get past the Rainbeye Monkeys" and so on. Instead, you've done it all by yourselves. Something you should all be very proud of. Well done!'

We all exchange glances.

'So,' continues Medwick, 'where was the telestone?'

The what?

'Sorry Medwick, the what?' I ask.

147

'The telestone. Sorry, I didn't explain, your uncle called his GCD 'the telestone' because it was a telephone that looked like a stone. Herf found it highly amusing!'

The girls giggle.

'Right, I see,' I say. 'We found it at the bottom of a trunk in a side room in The Dark Castle. We're heading along a corridor towards the West Tower at the moment.'

'Right,' says Medwick, 'seeing as we now have a way to communicate, I'm more than willing to help.' Finally! 'Reports are coming in that the Thargs are tightening security. Some kind of disturbance. Do they know that you're there, Eddie?'

'No, Medwick,' I reply, 'they definitely don't know that we're here.'

'What was the disturbance then?'

'It was Alan,' answers Becky.

'Alan! Who's Alan?'

'Our Ayck.'

'Your Ayck!! Eddie, please explain.'

I take a deep breath and explain.

# Chapter Fourteen

Now Medwick knows all that we've been through, we're all standing in a circle staring at the stone waiting for advice.

'You're waiting for me to advise you, aren't you Eddie?' comes Medwick's voice.

'Erm, I guess so,' I reply.

'See, I told you that you'd all start to do that once you had a GCD!' He did say that. 'What were you planning to do before you found the telestone?'

'Well,' I say, 'we worked out a route to the West Tower. Once there we were going to search for the formula and, well, take it from there!'

'Sounds like a good plan,' replies Medwick. 'No reason to change it, is there?'

I glance at the others.

'I guess not,' I say, 'it just looks a little simple. The route to the West Tower, that is.'

'Well,' replies Medwick,' I haven't spent much time in The Dark Castle, but it is a simple layout because many a Tharg would get lost if it was any more complicated. Terrible memories, most of the Thargs. But very dangerous. If you need any help from the Gingoile Special Guard, the Rainbeye Monkeys, the Aycks and even the leaves, now that they're walking again, just let me know.'

'You can get any or all of them to help us?' I ask.

'Well, apart from the Gingoile Special Guard, I can't guarantee anything. But I can ask and they all have grievances against the Thargs, so I would expect them to help.'

Raised eyebrows all around.

'Why would we need their help?' ventures Carrot with a quiver in his voice.

'Hopefully you won't, young Carrot, but if you do, just ask.'

'How do we use the telestone?' I ask.

'Just as you are now, Master Eddie,' replies Medwick, 'just hold it in your hand and talk. I will hear you and the people near you.'

'Will it only work if I hold it?' I ask.

'Krunk designed it for any Ross family member, so it will work for Liz as well.'

Liz looks at me and smiles. At least if something happens to me, Liz will still be able to contact Medwick.

'Right,' continues Medwick, 'I'm going to call a secret meeting of The Grand Order to see how we can assist you.'

'What's The Grand Order?' I ask.

'Delegates from every being in The Realm, except the Thargs of course. I shall ask them all to be on standby if you require them.'

'Why wasn't the meeting called earlier?' asks Liz.

'Because, young Liz, however secret we make the meeting, Thargs have ways of infiltrating. Look at the way they somehow managed to get that hologram of Zendorf into The Palace of the Realm. If they were aware of a meeting taking place before you got into The Dark Castle you wouldn't be where you are now. Now you are in there I feel it is worth taking the risk. Is that ok with you Master Eddie?'

'Er, I guess so, yes,' I reply.

'Fair enough,' continues Medwick. 'I'm pleased I can finally help all of you. It has been very difficult allowing you to continue with minimal help. But it is always the way with newcomers to The Realm. I hope you understand why it has to be this way.'

The others look at me and nod.

'I think I can speak for all of us that, although we've found it extremely difficult getting this far, we do understand why you have to do it this way. We're glad you can now help us if we need you.'

Phew! That was tricky to say! Liz puts her arm around my shoulders in support.

'Well done, Master Eddie!' says Medwick. 'Now, we've both got work to do. You know how to contact me if you need anything. Good luck!'

'Thanks, Medwick. And goodbye.' I reply.

The others say their goodbyes too, then I slide the telestone into my jacket pocket. I now have my box in one outer jacket pocket, the telestone in the other and the map in one of my inner pockets. I thought I'd never say this, but I could do with a jacket like Carrot's!

'Right then, Bro, shall we carry on to the West Tower?'

'Guess so,' I reply. 'Lead on, Brian.'

'Ok, Eddie.'

Brian gently unlatches the door and sniffs the air. I think he's exaggerating the sniff so that Liz realises he is constantly checking where we're going and not just diving in and out of each room willy-nilly!

'All clear.'

We file out and continue down the corridor. It's all very quiet. It is still dark outside, so I suppose most of the Thargs are in bed. That's as long as Thargs sleep at night and are awake during the day. Who knows! If they do sleep at night, I suppose there may be more patrols like the one we encountered a while ago. I guess I could have asked Medwick about the sleeping habits of the Thargs whilst I was on the telestone, but he did say he hadn't been in The Dark Castle much, so he may not have been able to help much.

'Here are the steps, Eddie,' whispers Brian.

'OK,' I reply. 'Keep going Brian.'

We go down a short spiral staircase and continue along the next corridor. Just up another few steps that we can all see at the end of this corridor and there will be the West Tower. Hopefully!

'Thargs!' exclaims Brian.

'Where?' I ask in a strained whisper.

'They're just about to come down the steps at the end of the corridor,' continues Brian. 'I can hear them.'

I can't hear a thing.

'Ok,' I say, 'if you say so, Brian. Take us into a safe side room.'

Brian goes to the nearest door, has a quick sniff of the air, and opens it.

'No Thargs in here!' announces Brian.

We quickly follow him in.

'Hide again,' I say as I crawl behind a chest of drawers.

I guess the others find a place to hide. I can't see them.

'Ok,' says Brian, 'they've gone!'

'Already?' I say as I stick my head above the chest of drawers. 'I'm sure I didn't hear them go past.'

'They didn't,' replied Brian, 'they got quite close and doubled back.'

We all look at Brian in amazement. How does he do it?

'Look at the map again, Eddie,' asks Liz, 'see if anything shows up on it in this room.'

'Ok,' I say as I remove the map from my pocket.

'Look,' says Carrot peering over my shoulder, 'another blue dot.'

He's right. The map's showing a small blue dot in the corner of the room.

'I'll look,' says Liz, heading towards the corner of the room.

'Anything there?' asks Becky.

'Nope,' replies Liz, 'except for a pebble!'

'Pick it up,' I say.

'Why?' replies Liz.

'I don't know,' I say. 'Pebble; stone… might be a connection?'

'But Medwick said that Krunk couldn't make a GCD smaller than the telestone,' says Carrot.

'True,' I reply, 'but pick it up anyway, Liz, and we'll at least see if the blue dot moves on my map.'

'Ok,' says Liz as she picks up the pebble. 'It's quite heavy for such a small pebble,' she continues as she starts walking towards me. 'Is the dot moving on the map?'

'I hope it is. I did put a tracker in it!'

'Erm,' stutters Carrot, 'who said that?'

'The pebble!' says Liz, looking down at her hand.

'But GCDs can't be that small,' replies Carrot.

'Who is this?' comes the voice from the stone.

'We could ask you the same!' I bravely reply, aiming my voice at the small pebble nestled in Liz's hand.

'If you were from The Realm,' continues the voice, 'you would recognise my voice.'

I look at the others. I can't reply. I can't say I'm not from The Realm. He might be a Tharg.

'And, if you're not from The Realm, maybe you've come to rescue me!?'

We all exchange frantic glances.

'Uncle Mark?' ventures Liz very tentatively, 'is that you?'

'Elizabeth?'

We all stop as one. Everyone looks at me, except Liz who I'm watching stare at the stone with tears welling in her eyes.

'Yes,' she replies. 'It's me; Elizabeth.'

'And Eddie?' the gentle voice asks from the pebble. 'Is Eddie with you?'

'Yes,' replies Liz, as she holds the pebble towards me, 'Eddie's here.'

'Hello, Eddie.'

'H... h... hello, Uncle Mark,' I stutter as the tears start to roll down Liz's cheeks.

'Eddie! I can't believe you've made it here!' he continues. 'Was it the box? Did you reach five feet up the wall?!'

'Yes. Yes, I did!' I say quite emphatically.

'I knew you would. It's in the genes! And how's my little sister?' he asks. 'Your mum. How's she?'

'She's great,' replies Liz, 'we're all great! I can't wait to tell Mum that you're no longer missing. That we've found you!'

'No, no,' replies Uncle Mark. 'You can't tell her where I am.'

'But why not?' asks Liz.

'It's dangerous,' replies our uncle. 'The fewer people who know of The Realm, the better.'

'But we could at least say you're alive,' I say. 'Without mentioning The Realm.'

'No, Eddie,' is his stern reply. 'If you start down that route you'll have to lie. That will lead to another lie and everything will start to unravel. If I ever get out of here I'll decide what to do about your mum, then.'

Liz dabs her tear-stained cheeks as we share a look.

'Oh, I wish I had time to have a proper long chat with you both,' Uncle Mark continues with real sadness in his voice, 'but I know my guard will be checking in on me again soon.'

'Ok,' I say firmly. We've only just found each other again, but we have work to do.

'What shall we do?' asks Liz. 'How do we save you?'

'Not me, dear Elizabeth,' says our uncle, 'save the formula. Did you get my holographic message?'

'Yes,' replies my sister.

'I explained it all there. It's going to have to be just the formula, Elizabeth.'

'But why?' pleads Liz.

'I'm assuming the disturbance by the Ayck was your doing?' asks Uncle Mark.

'It was,' I reply. 'Why?'

'Whenever there's any kind of disruption, or disturbance,' he replies, 'the guards are automatically doubled.'

'Really?' chips in Carrot. 'We have hardly seen any Thargs at all.'

'Whose voice is that?' asks my uncle.

'Oh, that's my best friend, Carrot,' I say realising that I haven't introduced everyone 'And then there's Becky and Brian,' I add.

'Hello, everyone,' says Uncle Mark.

'Hi,' is the brief reply from both Becky and Brian.

'The reason that you've not encountered many Thargs, Carrot, is because you're in the quietest part of the castle.'

'Oh,' says Carrot whilst throwing a shrug in my direction.

'You are near the West Tower,' he continues, 'whilst I'm in the North Tower and the formula is in the East Tower.'

Right. Well, at least we know where everything is!

'You said in your holographic message you didn't know where the formula was,' asks Liz.

'I didn't when I recorded that message. They move it around. It's definitely in the East Tower at the moment. Your disturbance will have doubled the guards near me and the formula.'

'We needed to create the disturbance to get in, Uncle,' says Liz, 'maybe we'd have done things differently if we'd known it would double the guard.'

'It's fully understandable, Elizabeth. The thing is you now need to create another distraction.'

'Really?' I say.

'Yes, Eddie.'

'Erm, ok.'

'But first, Eddie, are the leaves walking?'

'Yes,' I reply as I look round my friends' pensive faces glued to the pebble in Liz's hand. 'Why?'

'Because the leaves need to be walking to achieve anything in The Realm. I discovered that to my own cost.'

I'm now confronted by four pairs of eyes all clearly saying "what does that mean"!?

I'll take the plunge. 'What do you mean by that, Uncle?'

'I'm afraid I haven't got time to explain, Eddie,' comes his reply, 'but it's something on one of Medwick's scrolls, which Herf likes to read out. The Gingoiles' interpretation was wrong. I've had so much time to think things over whilst locked in here that I worked out that when you appear, the leaves should start walking and between them and you the formula should be successfully retrieved this time.'

Ok. Now everyone's looking really confused!

'This time?' pipes up Becky. 'You mean there have been other attempts to rescue you and the formula?'

'A few. But not for a long while. The Gingoiles' numbers are falling and the attacks are uncoordinated.'

'How can we make this one a success?' asks Liz.

'Has Medwick called a secret meeting of The Grand Order?'

'Yes; just now,' I reply.

'Listen carefully. My guard is on his way back. You must make sure Medwick tells The Grand Order that the leaves are walking. It is vital they know. Then they must send everyone possible to the North Tower, where I am. Make it look like they're trying to rescue me. Make a huge distraction. Then you and your friends, Eddie, must go back past the South Tower to the East Tower and get that formula. Damn.... He's here.... Must go....'

He's gone.

We all stare at the pebble. I look up at the others. If I didn't know it was a GCD, I'd have thought it very strange with all of us just staring at a pebble!

'Do you want this?' Liz eventually asks whilst offering me the pebble.

I pat my pockets, in the style of Carrot. 'I think I've got enough to carry already, Sis. Maybe you should keep that one.'

Liz silently puts the pebble in her pocket and wipes the remaining tears from her cheeks.

'What now?' offers Brian.

'Well,' I say somewhat tentatively, 'I guess we use the other GCD to tell Medwick what Uncle Mark has said and hope that The Grand Order can help us with the distraction.'

'And then what?' asks Liz. 'Even with the distraction, how do we get the formula from the East Tower?'

I have no idea.

'One step at a time,' I reply.

I can't say that I have no idea. Can I? I take out the stone-like GCD from my pocket and speak.

'Medwick, it's Eddie.' No reply. 'Medwick, it's Eddie.'

'Should you say "Over",' offers Carrot.

'I didn't last time. I just spoke,' I reply.

'Maybe he's busy sorting out the secret meeting,' says Becky.

'Or on the loo!?' blurts out Brian.

We all smile.

'Eddie, is that you?' comes a voice from the stone. It doesn't sound like Medwick.

'Who's that?' I ask.

'It's Herf.'

'Hello Herf. Where's Medwick?'

'He's chairing a secret meeting of The Grand Order,' is Herf's reply.

'Already?' I say. 'That was quick!'

'We may look like we're built for comfort, Eddie,' replies a slightly flustered Herf, 'but we can act with great speed when necessary!'

We all share smiles, once more.

'I really need to talk to Medwick, Herf. I've spoken to Uncle Mark and he has given me some important information to pass on.'

'You've spoken to him!?' replies an excited Herf. 'Oh my, oh my, wait there. I'll get Medwick to get back to you as soon as I can. Wait there, Eddie!'

'Ok, Herf, I'll wait!' I say in as calm a way as possible.

Liz and Becky can't help but share a small chuckle at the over-excited Herf.

'I wonder how they communicate,' offers Carrot after a moment of silence.

'Communi – what?' asks Brian.

We're now used to Brian's random questioning of words.

'Talking,' replies Carrot, 'I wonder how they all talk to each other?'

'Who?' asks Liz.

'All the members of The Grand Order,' continues Carrot.

'How do you mean?' asks Becky.

'Well,' continues Carrot, 'The Grand Order contains delegates from all beings in The Realm, according to Medwick.'

'Except the Thargs,' adds Liz.

'Yes,' says Carrot, 'and so far, we know of Gingoiles, Rainbeye Monkeys and Aycks. How do they all talk to each other?'

'Can Rainbeye Monkeys talk?' adds Becky. 'And as for Aycks, they just make a racket!'

We all chuckle.

'A racket I can translate!' comes a voice.

'Medwick?' asks Liz as I lift the pebble lying in my hand a little higher.

'Yes, Liz. I'm here!' comes the reply.

'They all have their own languages?' asks Liz.

'Oh, yes,' comes the reply, 'and many of us can converse in many languages. But, now's not the time, Liz. I need to speak to Eddie most urgently.'

'I'm here, Medwick,' I say.

157

'Now then, Master Eddie,' says Medwick in what can only be described as a more serious voice, 'Herf informs me that you've spoken with your uncle. Is that true?'

'Yes,' I say, 'just now. We found a GCD of his and have made contact.'

'What did he say?' asks Medwick.

'He said that you need to ask The Grand Order to agree to make a huge distraction near the North Tower, where he is, so that we can attempt to get the formula from the East Tower.'

'I need more than that, Eddie,' continues Medwick, 'the meeting hasn't started well and I won't get support for an action like that. We've tried that before and it failed. More than once.'

'Uncle Mark says that it needs to be coordinated better,' I say.

'Your uncle needs to realise that we do our best!' comes the disgruntled reply.

'He does,' I say quickly, 'and this time we're already inside the castle walls, so it must be easier to coordinate?'

'That's still not enough, I'm afraid.'

'The leaves,' whispers Liz, 'tell him about the leaves.'

'Who's that whispering?' asks Medwick.

'Just Liz,' I say, 'reminding me to tell you that the leaves are walking.'

'I know they are,' replies Medwick, 'and I've already told The Grand Order they are. But that's still not enough!'

'But Uncle Mark believes there's huge significance in the fact they are walking again at the same time as us being here.'

'Really?' replies Medwick. 'I suppose it *could* be more than a coincidence.'

'It is,' I continue. 'Uncle Mark says there's an old scroll which the Gingoiles have misinterpreted and that he's figured out.'

'Really?'

'Yes. He didn't say which scroll. One which mentions the leaves, I guess. You need to reinterpret it and use that to convince The Grand Order to help.'

The voice from the pebble goes quiet. I look around at the others. Nobody says anything.

'I've sent Herf for the scrolls,' says Medwick after a short while. 'I shall study them along with the rest of The Grand Order.'

'Do you think that might be enough to get their help?' I ask.

'It's possible,' replies Medwick. 'We'll be as open-minded as we can in reinterpreting things.'

'Ok,' I reply.

'Until then, Eddie, I suggest you all carefully make your way to the East Tower in preparation.'

'Ok, Medwick,' I say, 'we will.'

'I'll be back in touch as soon as I can.'

I slip the stone back into my pocket as we all seem to draw breath as one.

'To the East Tower then, Bro?'

'Yes, Liz,' I reply, 'via the South Tower. Not the North!'

'I know,' replies Liz with a disconsolate shrug.

'Shall I lead the way, Eddie,' asks Brian.

'Yes, please,' I reply.

Brian unlatches the door, takes a brief sniff, and leads us back the way we came.

*

That wasn't too difficult. We briefly hid in a side room near the South Tower to allow a couple of patrolling Thargs to wander past. The rest has been pretty quiet. We've checked the map a couple of times, but Carrot's quite confident that he's got the route clear in his head.

'Is that side room empty, Brian?' asks Carrot.

Brian heads to the room and places his ear on the door. He then slowly lifts the latch and gives his now customary sniff.

'All clear,' he says as he disappears inside. We all follow him in. It's yet another plain room with only a smattering of furniture.

'Why have we come in here, Carrot?' asks Becky.

'Because the East Tower is not far, now,' comes the reply. 'I think it's just around a couple of bends and I don't think we should get any closer without the disturbance at the North Tower because there's bound to be a lot more Thargs around those couple of bends! Can I check the map please, Eddie?'

'Of course,' I reply as I retrieve the map and hand it to him.

'I'm right,' says Carrot as he peers at the map which has, once more, changed itself so it's showing the correct part of The Dark Castle. 'A bend, a door, a short straight passage, followed by another bend and door. Then the East Tower.'

'Could you sense any Thargs ahead, Brian?' asks Liz. Brian looks down at the map in Carrot's hands.

'No,' he replies, 'but I think if we went through one more door I might get more of an idea.'

'Should we go through one more door, Eddie?' asks my sis.

I look around before I reply.

'I think we're close enough. We don't want to risk making ourselves known until we have to. I think we should wait here until Medwick gets back to us. Agreed?'

'Agreed!' comes the unanimous reply.

Smiles are shared as we all find places to sit. I sit on a three-legged stool. It's quite uncomfortable. Each of the legs on the stool are different lengths. How bizarre!

I look at the rest of my team. Family, friends and Brian. That's not fair. I guess Brian's a friend and if he wasn't one before, he certainly is now!

'Is your stool as uncomfortable as mine?' asks Carrot as he places his four-legged stool down next to mine and sits on it. 'All the legs are different lengths!'

He sits and wobbles.

'Yes, it is!' I reply as I begin to wobble on my three-legged excuse for a stool.

We both start to laugh.

'Ssh!' says Becky. 'We'll be discovered if you two keep laughing.'

'Quite right,' I reply as we stop wobbling.

'It's ok, Becky,' says Brian who's placed himself by the door, 'there's no one out there.'

'Even so...' replies Becky.

'No. You're right, Becky,' I say.

'Nice to see you laughing, Eddie,' says Liz, 'not been too much to laugh about since we've been here, has there?'

'Guess not,' I reply as I make my way over to Liz and put my arm around her.

It goes quiet for a few seconds.

'Well,' starts up Carrot, 'at least we now know why the Thargs are always patrolling.'

'Because they've got my uncle locked in one tower and the formula in the other?'

'No,' replies Carrot as he stands up, 'because their furniture is so uncomfortable to sit on!'

We all laugh.

'Ssh,' says Becky, again.

'Sorry!' I reply as we all quieten down.

'No, not because we might be heard, but because I think I can hear a voice.'

We stop and listen. I can hear a low-level cough. It sounds like someone clearing their throat.

'It's Medwick on the telestone,' says Brian.

'So it is,' I say as I pull the GCD from my pocket. 'Hello?'

'Ah,' comes Medwick's voice from the stone, 'finished all your laughing, have you?'

'Yes,' I say as I look around at all the others, 'sorry.'

'No need to apologise to me, Master Eddie, I just hope you're taking this seriously!'

'Of course, we are,' I reply.

'I hope so,' says a stern sounding Medwick. 'You do realise your merriment may be heard by the Thargs and the whole plan will fail!'

'It's just a laugh,' replies Liz before I can find any words. 'Brian's keeping an eye out and we had a laugh. Now; what's the plan?'

Liz pats me on the arm. Thanks, Sis.

'Right, well,' comes the slightly flustered response from Medwick, 'Krank has re-deciphered the scroll.'

'Krank?' questions Carrot, 'don't you mean Krunk?'

'No, no young Carrot,' replies Medwick, 'Krunk's no good with words; he's machines! His younger brother, Krank, is the one who has a way with words.'

'Oh, right,' replies Carrot.

'And what did he manage to re-decipher?' I ask.

'Ah, well,' comes the unusually stuttering reply from Medwick, 'Krank informs me that the past-participle of the outer sanctum was pre-dispositionally opposed to the inner curve of the primary function which, when placed hexodesimically from the adjunctive verb, caused the derata stratum to not be considered correctly.'

We all share extremely bemused looks.

'Wow,' exclaims Carrot, 'you remembered all that?'

'Erm, no,' comes Medwick's reply, 'Krank wrote it down for me!'

We now share smiles.

'And what does it mean?' I venture.

'It means, Master Eddie, that the leaves only walk when necessary. And when they do walk, we must use their help to achieve our goals.'

'Which is getting the formula,' I reply.

'Exactly. So; are you in position?'

'Yes,' I reply, 'we feel that we're as close to the East Tower as we can be without being seen.'

'Excellent!' replies Medwick, 'then, very soon, you will hear a commotion. Then you advance and retrieve the formula.'

'You make it sound easy,' says Becky.

'Did I, young Becky?' replies Medwick. 'I didn't mean to. But, the size of the commotion should draw virtually every Tharg out to defend the North Tower.'

'Should?' asks Carrot.

'I beg your pardon, young Carrot?'

'You said "should", meaning it might not.'

162

'True, true. We'll do our best to distract them all, but you should be prepared to encounter *some* Thargs.'

Carrot visibly gulps.

'How are you going to get every Tharg in The Dark Castle to head towards the North Tower?' I ask.

'The leaves and Aycks are planning on dropping the Gingoile Special Guard and the Rainbeye Monkeys into the vicinity of the North Tower. Then they'll do all the frightful things they're capable of – and I'm certainly not – and when you have the formula, you're to make your way to the nearest exit by the East Tower, which takes you onto the top of the battlements. The leaves and Aycks will be looking out for you and will whisk you away.'

'Right,' is all I can manage to say.

'Now, I must go and make sure everything this end is as organised as possible. Take care, all of you.'

'Thank you, Medwick,' I reply on behalf of everyone, 'and when will the distraction start?'

'Soon, Master Eddie, soon....'

# Chapter Fifteen

"Soon" keeps running through my head as we look at maps and try to make plans.

'This is ridiculous,' says Liz, 'we've no idea how many Thargs are going to be in between here and the East Tower, have we?'

'I suppose not,' I reply.

'We're just going to have to trust Medwick when he says that the distraction should draw most of the Thargs towards the North Tower,' says Becky.

'We need to have some plans prepared, just in case,' I say. 'We can't just blunder forward without any plans.'

'I don't think we should be going forward at all,' says Carrot.

'Pardon?' I question.

'We'll be heading into the unknown,' continues Carrot. 'We need to draw them out and draw them into our traps.'

'Such as?' asks Liz.

'Well, the corridors are dimly lit, aren't they, Brian.'

'Yes,' he replies.

'Well,' continues Carrot as he removes the thin cord we used at the waterfall from his pocket, 'between the dim corridor and the dim Thargs, we should be able to use the cord as tripwires along the corridor. Draw them out, trip them up.'

'Then what?' asks Becky.

'What do you mean?' replies Carrot.

'The tripped up Tharg gets up again and kills us?'

'Oh,' says Carrot, 'I see what you mean. I hadn't thought of that. I was just hoping they'd knock themselves out from falling over!'

'Possible,' says Becky, 'but unlikely.'

'If they get up again,' says Brian, 'I'll just thump them!'

'Are you sure?' I ask.

'Sure,' replies Brian, 'I can do that. It's what I do!'

We all chuckle.

'I think I'll arm myself with this,' announces Brian as he strides across the room and picks up the stool I'd vacated. 'It'll do nicely,' he continues as he yanks one of the legs from the stool and whacks it into his open palm as if his hand is a Tharg's head!

'Blimey, Brian,' says Liz, 'steady on!'

'It's us or them, now, Liz,' replies Brian as he whacks the wooden leg into his open palm once more. 'Us or them.'

'Eddie?' says Liz, 'is this necessary?'

'Well,' I say, 'I think it should be our last resort and I think the most it would do is knock a Tharg out. I really don't think it could kill one. Could it?'

Brian holds the relatively spindly leg up.

'I doubt it,' he says.

'If it's as good as a weapon as it is at being a stool leg,' says Carrot, 'it'll be useless!'

'That's true,' says Brian as he starts to pull out another stool leg, 'I'd better take a spare!'

We all laugh, again.

'Last resort, though, Brian,' I say, 'if they trip and stay down, leave them alone. Only hit them if they start to get up again.'

'Right, Eddie,' replies Brian as he waves two legs around like an ill-trained Samurai, 'got it.'

'Right,' says Carrot, whilst looking at the map, 'we need to go through the next door and lay the tripwire on the short straight passage. Then, when any Tharg exits the East Tower in this direction they'll run round the bend and not see the tripwires. You can hide in the alcove here, Brian, and bop them on the head, or whatever, if they stand up again. OK?'

'Yep,' says Brian as he takes in Carrot's instructions.

'What are me and Becky doing?' asks Liz

'Well,' continues Carrot, 'seeing as the North Tower is in the other direction from the East Tower, I'm not expecting any Thargs to come this way.'

'Oh,' says Becky.

'So,' continues Carrot, 'you need to draw any Thargs out that are left in the East Tower.'

'Ok,' replies Liz. 'How?'

'Erm...' says Carrot.

A few seconds pass.

'Knock down ginger!' exclaims Brian.

'What?' says Liz.

'Knock down ginger,' repeats Brian. 'My dad says he used to do it when he was younger.'

'Do what?' I ask.

'Knock on people's front doors,' continues Brian, 'and run away!'

We all look at each other.

'Why?' ventures Liz

'He said it was fun!' says Brian.

'Ok,' I say, 'fair enough. Even though I can't see the fun in that, it should work.'

'What...? Me and Becky just knock on the door and run away?'

'Yes,' answers Brian.

'It'd only need one of you,' says Carrot.

'I think we'd be better together, don't you Becky? Just in case?'

'Yes,' comes the firm reply from Becky.

'So,' continues Liz. 'Me and Becky knock and run...'

'Carefully avoiding the tripwires once you've come round the bend,' interjects Carrot.

'... Brian bops them on the head...'

'If necessary,' adds Carrot.

'... and what are you doing Carrot?'

'Well,' replies Carrot. 'Having set the tripwires I'll wait in here with Eddie.'

We all look at him.

'Someone's got to protect Eddie,' says Carrot, 'haven't they?'

'Well, yes, I suppose so,' says Liz.

'Hang on,' I say, 'I can't just sit here whilst you're all running around and bopping Thargs on the head, can I!?

'We still need to protect you, Bro.'

'I know, Liz, but I brought you all here. You're all doing this because of me. I need to do something!'

Nobody speaks.

'Plus,' I continue, 'I can't just sit and wait here. Once we get the formula we need to get outside as quickly as possible so we can be rescued by the leaves and Aycks. There won't be time to run back and collect me and Carrot and then get up onto the battlements.'

'You've got a point, Eddie,' says my sis. 'Maybe you and Carrot could just bring up the rear? Follow us at a little distance?'

'How's that sound, Carrot?' I ask.

'OK,' he replies, 'I suppose we could bring up the rear, and cover the rear, just in case a rogue Tharg is coming the other way.'

'Good,' I say, 'that's agreed, then. Now we've no idea how long we've got, so let's go and lay the tripwire. Lead the way, Brian.'

'Right you are, Eddie.'

\*

Ten minutes later we're done. Brian got us to the short passage before the final bend and door to the East Tower. We could hear Tharg noises beyond that door, so we're just hoping they run towards the North Tower when the commotion starts. Carrot has laid the tripwire across the passageway and Liz and Becky have plotted their route through it so that they avoid tripping when running from the door. Brian's in his alcove, armed with his bits of wood, and I'm watching from the back.

'I think that's it,' announces Carrot as we both look at the zigzag of thin rope across the corridor.

'Do you think it will hold?' I ask.

'Most of it should,' replies Carrot. 'The walls are all jagged rock, so there were plenty of places to hook the rope.'

'Good,' I reply.

'Right,' I announce to everyone in a loud whisper, 'once the disturbance starts, we'll give the Thargs a minute or two to head away from the East Tower to the North and then Liz and Becky can knock on the door and run back this way.'

'Ok, Bro.'

'And then,' I continue, 'I guess we make the rest up as we go along!?'

'We're getting good at that,' says Carrot who pats me on the back.

'Ok,' I say, 'let's just wait quietly. It can't be long now.'

'Here,' says Carrot after a few seconds, 'take these.'

'Darts?' I say as I take three shiny, new darts from my friend. 'Why on earth have you got a set of darts in one of your pockets?'

'They're your birthday present,' replies Carrot. 'I bought them the other day for you and accidentally left them in one of my pockets.'

'They're brilliant, mate,' I say as I look at the shiny barrels and orange flights. 'Luton colours, as well!'

'Yep,' replies Carrot.'

'But, why give them to me now?' I ask.

'Defence!' comes Carrot's reply.

'Defence!?'

'I was thinking,' continues Carrot, 'that we're bringing up the rear and don't have any weapons. That's when I remembered the darts.'

'Good thinking. Why don't you keep them?' I ask.

'You're better at darts than me,' replies Carrot.

'Not really,' I say.

'Seventeen legs to three says you are,' says Carrot, smiling.

'Blimey; is that the score?'

'Yep,' replies Carrot, 'that's why I've given you the darts.'

'Right.'

'Happy Birthday for next week, by the way!'

'Don't say that now,' I say, 'makes it sound like one of us won't be around next week!'

'You never know,' says Carrot, sadly.

'We'll all be at my birthday party next week,' I say putting my arm around Carrot's shoulders, 'and you take one dart and if you need to use it think of that double top you got that one time.'

'Ok,' says Carrot as he accepts the dart from me, 'and you remember that treble nineteen; bull!'

'I'll never forget that,' I say as I look down at the two darts I'm left holding.

'Thanks for my birthday present, Carrot.'

'You're welcome, Eddie. I'll give you the final third of it in a little while!'

We both laugh.

'What's that?' calls out Brian in a loud whisper from his alcove.

'What?' I reply.

'That noise,' he continues. 'I think the Aycks are coming!'

'Anyone else hear them?' I venture.

'Yes,' says Becky, 'I can. I hope Alan's ok.'

'I'm sure he's fine,' says Liz comfortingly.

'Yep!' I exclaim, 'I can hear them too.'

'So can the Thargs!' adds Carrot as a siren starts up. 'They didn't use the siren when they saw Alan, earlier.'

'I'm guessing, well hoping, there's a lot more than Alan this time!' I say.

'What now?' asks Liz, raising her voice over the siren.

'Keep an eye in that direction,' I say whilst pointing at our target.

Everyone starts to look pensive.

'It sounds like the Thargs are leaving the East Tower,' says Becky whilst edging towards the final bend. 'Shall we knock and run now?'

'Liz?' I say. 'What do you think?'

'Now's as good a time as any!' she replies with a smile.

I can't bring myself to tell my sister and Becky to head towards danger, so I just nod. Liz understands and heads around the final bend with Becky by her side. She's now out of my sight.

'Have they knocked, yet?' asks Carrot.

'I've no idea,' I reply. 'I can't hear over the siren.'

'Brian,' I call, 'have they knocked yet?'

Brian nods.

How does he do it?!

'Two!' comes the huge cry from Liz. 'Two!'

She's still out of sight, but we all know they'll be with us any moment, followed by two Thargs.

I look at Brian. He nods once more and changes his stance.

Round the corner comes Becky, followed by Liz. They're running quite quickly; but not as quick as I thought they would be!

'They're a little way behind,' calls Becky as she nimbly skips over the twine.

'They're not the quickest!' exclaims Liz as she follows Becky's route.

A few seconds later a Tharg who, quite frankly, is overweight, lumbers into view. He is holding some sort of short-handled club and he has his eyes fixed on Liz and Becky, who are getting towards the end of the maze of twine. Even though the Tharg is hardly lifting his feet off the floor, he manages to clear the first couple of lengths of twine. But, the third length snares him. He staggers a few more yards (metres!) before his top-heavy bulk forces him down. The crash is really quite epic. His head smacks the floor pretty hard. Brian goes to move from his alcove, but I shake my head. Brian knows what I mean.

'There's the second one!' calls Liz over the tedious siren.

This one is possibly more overweight than the first! I'm sure the Thargs we encountered by the well near Flounge's house were nimbler? Maybe the larger Thargs are put on static duty? Standing next to the formula? Clearly these Thargs are not built for speed!

This Tharg pauses for a moment to take in the scene. He sees his colleague flat on the floor and looks at Liz and Becky who have stopped this side of the twine. They're still a little way from me and Carrot. He then looks at the maze of twine. Damn! If he'd been on the heels of the other Tharg he'd have probably tripped over the twine. But, being a bit further back has bought him some time and lost us our element of surprise. He looks menacingly towards Liz and Becky and starts to swing his club around in front of him as he picks his way across the twine.

'What now, Eddie!?' calls out Becky.

Before I can answer, the Tharg stops walking and readjusts his gaze towards me and Carrot.

'Eddie?' says the Tharg.

Liz and Becky stare across at me in amazement. I can see Brian in his alcove also staring at me – mouth open.

'How does he know your name?' whispers Carrot, who is still by my side.

'Because Becky just told him!' I reply.

'I know that!' says Carrot, 'but he's saying it as if he's heard your name before!'

'Maybe he has,' I reply, 'maybe Uncle Mark has warned them of me!?'

'Would he put you in danger by telling them of you?' asks Carrot with a shrug.

'No, you're right. Probably not.'

'Eddie Ross?' says the Tharg.

Ok. This is now getting weird.

'I don't know how,' says Carrot, 'but he's *definitely* heard of you!'

'Yes,' I say as I take a step away from Carrot, 'I am Eddie Ross!'

'What are you doing Eddie!?' cries out Liz.

Yes…. What am I doing?

'Well,' I venture, 'he seems to speak English, so I thought I'd try and talk him out of hitting us with that club!'

'Eddie Ross!' says the Tharg with a little more menace than I'd anticipated. 'Jointle sprak gundra dee. Harkel tront zed.'

'I don't think he speaks English, Bro, I think he just knows your name.'

'Erm, yes,' I stutter.

'Ung mertal, Eddie Ross, harf ren kumpf, Eddie Ross!'

The Tharg has changed direction. He's heading towards me.

'Ung mertal, Eddie Ross, harf ren kumpf, Eddie Ross!' he repeats.

'What's he saying?' asks Becky.

'I don't know,' I reply, 'but I don't like it!'

The Tharg is making good progress through the twine. He's now past Brian, in his alcove. This gives me an idea. I look at Brian, who still looks up for the fight, and I give him a nod and a sideways glance. Brian, through his sixth sense which we all now know he's got, starts to creep up behind the Tharg. Carrot starts to back away behind me.

Closer, Brian. Closer.

'Ung mertal, Eddie Ross, harf ren kumpf, Eddie Ross!' continues the Tharg.

Thwack! Brian clobbers the Tharg over his head. The spindly stool leg breaks into two on the Tharg's thick skull. He immediately turns to face Brian. He seems initially surprised by the size of Brian, but then starts to raise his club above his head. Suddenly a dart whistles over my head.

'Double top,' I hear Carrot cry from behind me.

The dart hits the back of the Tharg's head. There's a cry of pain from the Tharg who turns and faces me once more. I feel like pointing at Carrot and saying 'it wasn't me,' but I don't think that would be helpful!

Thwack! Brian hits the Tharg again, with his spare stool leg. This leg is definitely sturdier than the first as the Tharg appears to black out immediately and crumple to the floor.

'Nice one, Brian,' calls out Becky.

'It wasn't just me,' says Brian as he lifts his head up from studying his prey, 'it was Carrot's dart which…'

Brian fades away and points over my shoulder to where Carrot should be standing. We all turn to look.

Carrot is being held firm by a Tharg. A much leaner looking Tharg. He has one hand over Carrot's mouth and one round his waist. In fact, Carrot's being held off the floor. He's not even struggling. The hand over the mouth, combined with the tight grip on his waist, seem to be squeezing the air out of Carrot.

'Herntal quime, Eddie Ross,' says the Tharg as he backs away from us.

'Put him down,' I say quite ineffectually.

'Herntal quime, Eddie Ross,' repeats the Tharg.

'Leave him alone!' calls out Becky as tears start to stream down her face.

'He's not armed,' says Brian who is heading towards me, 'let me attack him.'

'No,' I say, 'he's squeezing the breath out of Carrot. He'll be dead before you reach them.'

'Herntal quime, Eddie Ross,' comes the Tharg once more.

'Why does he keep repeating your name?' asks Brian. 'Doesn't he know he's got Carrot?'

Hang on! That's it!

'No,' I say, 'I don't think he knows he's got Carrot. I think that he thinks he's got me!'

'What?' says my sis.

'He probably heard the other Tharg saying my name,' I continue, 'came round the corner, saw Carrot throw the dart and thought he'd got me!'

'So, what do we do?' asks Becky who's trying to stop her tears by wiping her eyes on her sleeve.

'Do the same as me,' I announce.

'I'm Eddie Ross,' I say whilst pointing at my chest and gingerly taking a step towards the Tharg, 'I'm Eddie Ross.'

'No; I'm Eddie Ross,' joins in Liz.

That's it, Sis.

'I'm Eddie Ross,' says Brian from behind me.

'Herntal quime, Eddie Ross,' says the Tharg, once more.

'No; I'm Eddie Ross,' exclaims Becky.

The Tharg seems to slightly relax his grip as some sort of confusion takes over.

'I'm Eddie Ross,' I repeat.

The others keep repeating the phrase.

Just a bit looser, Tharg. Just a bit looser....

Now! I grab my darts.

'Double nineteen!'

I shout as I aim for the Tharg's right knee cap. There's a cry of pain as I hit my target. He drops Carrot in a heap.

'Bull!' I holler as I launch my final dart towards the Tharg's stomach. 'Gotcha!'

The Tharg doubles over. As he does, Brian runs past me and clobbers him on the back of his head with his sturdy stool leg. The leg remains in one piece as the Tharg collapses to the floor. We all rush to Carrot who is, thankfully, starting to sit up.

'You ok, mate?' I ask.

'I'm alright, Eddie,' replies Carrot. 'I'm Spartacus!'

We all laugh, knowingly.

'What?' asks Brian.

'Just a film, Brian,' says Becky. 'We'll show you it one day.'

'Ok,' replies Brian. 'Cool!'

I help Carrot up as Brian retrieves the darts and Liz and Becky collect our knapsacks and the twine.

'Here are your darts, Eddie,' says Brian.

'Thanks, Brian,' I reply.

'Can you keep them in one of your pockets for me, please, Carrot?' I ask as I hold out the three darts.

'Sure, mate,' he replies. 'I might even wrap them for your birthday!'

\*

We're all sorted. Everything recovered and put away. Three Thargs tied up with the twine and dragged into the side room we were in earlier. The siren has stopped, but the battle is clearly continuing outside. The sounds are horrific. The sooner we're on the battlements waiting to be picked up, the sooner the Gingoile Special Guard and Rainbeye Monkeys, and anyone else who has put their life at risk for us, can retreat from The Dark Castle.

We're now staring down the final corridor, looking at the door Liz and Becky knocked on. A door which was left open by the two Thargs which chased them.

'What do you reckon, Brian?' I ask. 'Tharg-free in there?'

'Yep,' he replies. 'Tharg-free in there.'

We follow Brian into the East Tower.

Carrot locks the door behind us and goes to check the other door.

'Right,' says Carrot, 'we're locked in.'

'Great,' says Becky.

'And the steps to the battlements are through that door?' asks Liz whilst pointing at the door Carrot has just checked.

'Yep!' comes his reply.

'So,' says Brian, 'where's this formula?'

We all look around. The room is completely empty. All the rooms in this castle are pretty empty. But this is completely empty.

'Nothing!' says Liz. 'There is absolutely nothing in here!'

'It must be in the West Tower,' offers Becky.

'But Uncle Mark says it's here, in the East Tower,' replies Liz.

'Maybe they moved it when the sirens went off,' says Carrot.

'Or maybe it's hidden in here?' I say. 'We must check this room thoroughly before heading anywhere else.'

'We don't have time to go anywhere else, Eddie,' says Carrot. 'If it's not here we have to get to the battlements and leave. Empty handed.'

Everyone looks downbeat.

'It must be here,' I say, trying to rally my troops. 'Check the walls, floor, everything.'

Everyone spreads out and starts feeling the walls and floor.

Cold stone. Everywhere.

'What's that?' says Brian after a few seconds.

'What?' I say.

'That tapping,' replies Brian.

We all stop.

'It's over here,' says Brian as he moves along the wall a little way. 'Ssh.'

We all stand motionless near the noise.

'Lever,' comes a faint voice seeming to emanate from solid stone.

'Where?' replies Brian, who seems happy to take on the challenge.

'Gap in stone. Three along,' is the reply.

'There!' exclaims Becky whilst pointing at a gap between two stones; three along from the voice.

'Shall I see if there's a lever in there, Eddie?' asks Brian.

'I guess so,' I reply.

'What if it's a trap?' asks Carrot.

'I think that person's in the trap,' I reply. 'I don't think we've a lot of choice, do you?'

'Guess not,' answers Carrot.

'Go on, Brian; see if you can find a lever.'

'Ok, Eddie,' says Brian as he places his thumb in the gap. 'I think I've found something.'

Suddenly the seamless wall shifts and slides to reveal a very old Gingoile sitting on a wooden stool in a very confined space.

'Hello,' says the old Gingoile.

'Hello,' I say, 'I'm Eddie.'

'Hello, Eddie,' he replies, 'I've been expecting you.'

I look around at my friends who, like me, seem surprised by this admission.

'Have you?' I ask.

'Oh, yes,' comes the reply.

'And who are you? I continue.

'Me?' he says. 'I'm the formula!'

# Chapter Sixteen

Silence. Except for a huge battle raging outside. A battle which snaps me back to my senses.

'I don't understand,' I say. 'But we don't have time for explanations now. If you really are what we came here for, we need to get out of here as soon as possible to put an end to the battle going on out there.'

'I agree,' replies the Gingoile.

'I don't think I'm following this anymore,' says Brian.

'It's alright, Brian,' says Becky, 'I don't think any of us are.'

'Oh!'

'Right, Brian,' I say, 'lead the way. Out of that door and up the steps to the battlements.'

'Ok, Eddie,' replies Brian as he unlocks the door, lifts the latch, has a quick sniff and heads out of the room.'

'Do you need to take anything?' I say to the Gingoile.

'No,' he replies, 'everything I need is in here.'

He leaves the room tapping his forehead.

Thankfully the route to the battlements is quite straightforward and clear of Thargs. As we reach the top, we can see that the battle at the North Tower isn't going well. If the Thargs were caught by surprise, they've managed to reorganise themselves. The relatively small Rainbeye Monkeys are standing as tall as they can with their eyes blazing red. They continue to fight in an ordered fashion; karate-like moves. But there is a solid line of Thargs, hidden behind shields, gradually forcing them away – thankfully towards the West Tower and not where we're standing, on top of the East. Various Gingoiles, who I assume are the Special Guard, are involved in a slightly less organised way than the monkeys, but they're also being pushed back. Occasional arrows and spears come down on the brave Gingoiles and monkeys and there are clearly some casualties.

'I can't watch,' cries Becky.

Liz and Brian comfort her.

The Aycks are circling, making their noise. Most of the Thargs seem to be wearing headphones, although some seem to be struggling with the noise. Hopefully that's our little bit of handiwork which is causing some discomfort.

'What now?' asks Carrot.

Before I can answer, a swirl of leaves rises from outside the castle and forms a huge star above our heads. This signal causes the Gingoile Special Guard and Rainbeye Monkeys to break ranks and run towards the West Tower. The Aycks and leaves split into two. Most of them head towards the West Tower whilst three large Aycks and swathes of leaves head for us.

'Watch out!' says the rescued Gingoile, 'Aycks are better landing on water than land and there's not a lot of room up here!'

We all move to the sides as the overgrown swan-like Aycks crash land among us on the battlements. They quickly recover and start making their slightly uncomfortable noise.

'Get on, then,' says the Gingoile.

'What?' I say.

'That's what they're saying,' continues the Gingoile. '"Please get on!" they're saying. One of you on each Ayck.'

'Ok,' says Brian setting off for the nearest Ayck.

'Not you,' blurts out the Gingoile, 'they do have a weight limit, you know!'

'Oh, sorry,' replies the slightly embarrassed Brian.

'You three must get on the Aycks,' instructs the Gingoile whilst pointing at Liz, Becky and Carrot.

'What about the rest of you?' asks Liz.

'The leaves will take care of us,' replies the Gingoile whilst looking at the leaves swirling above our heads.

'Quick, now,' says the Gingoile, 'the Thargs are now heading this way.'

He's right. The Thargs have split into two. Half are following the retreating Special Guard and monkeys, and the rest have spotted us and are making their way along the battlements towards us. This half is headed by Zendorf. We may have only seen his hologram before, but I recognise him.

'Quickly,' I say as I point along the battlements, 'it's Zendorf!'

Everyone turns and visibly gulps as one. The hologram was kind to Zendorf. He's definitely more terrifying in real life and his presence makes everyone speed up!

'See you soon, Bro,' says Liz as she mounts the Ayck and grabs hold of its neck.

The beast squawks.

'Not too tight round the neck, Miss,' says the Gingoile.

'Sorry,' replies my sis as she loosens her grip.

'Bye,' all three of them cry as the Aycks take off with their passengers. They initially drop out of sight, below the battlements, before rising again and heading away from The Dark Castle.

'Now, our turn!' says the Gingoile as the leaves all fall onto the floor in between me, Brian and the Gingoile. I really must ask him his name!

'On you get,' says the Gingoile as he steps on the leaves and sits down.

Brian and I shrug at each other and do likewise.

'Krantel brimf unk himtoe!' cries Zendorf as he closes in on us.

'What does that mean?' I ask.

'Well,' replies the Gingoile, 'most of it was, quite frankly, unnecessary swearing. But, basically, he was shouting "attack"!'

A spear whistles between mine and Brian's heads.

'Aaghh,' cries out Brian.

'Time to fly, please, leaves!' announces the Gingoile.

With that the leaves rise as one. Just like a magic carpet. All spongy and soft just like when we walked on them earlier.

Suddenly, more spears are whistling around our heads.

'We're a bit of an obvious target, leaves,' says the Gingoile, 'can we split into three, do you think?'

Immediately our large magic carpet splits into three small ones. Brian's immediately drops lower (probably because he's the heaviest), the Gingoile's carpet stays around the same height and mine goes higher.

'They won't catch us now!' shouts the old Gingoile, who clearly has a new lease of life now we're flying away from The Dark Castle.

'Lerso pok junf, Zendorf,' shouts out the Gingoile.

'What does that mean?' I shout.

'Just politely saying goodbye!' replies the Gingoile.

Politely? Really!?

The spears stop being thrown. The castle fades away behind us and we start to catch up with the Aycks.

*

We can hear the cheers as we come to land on the lawn outside The Palace of the Realm. Gingoiles everywhere. Our leaves land gently for us. Unfortunately, even though they do their best, the Aycks tumble on landing throwing Liz, Becky and Carrot clear. They're quickly gathered in by concerned Gingoiles. They look like they're all laughing, though!

'Bumpy landing?' I ask.

'Just a bit,' replies Carrot as Liz and Becky give each other a hug.

'Let Medwick through,' says Herf as he jostles his way through the crowd, 'let Medwick through!'

'Alright, Herf,' replies Medwick, 'I can manage.'

Herf stops near me, but doesn't speak and Medwick rushes by, ignoring both me and the rescued Gingoile. What's going on!?

Ah, I see now. Medwick is approaching our transportation. He stops and bows before the three Aycks. There is a raucous reply before they take off and glide away. He then turns to the leaves, which have rejoined as one carpet since we got off them. For the leaves, Medwick takes to his knees before bowing. The leaves do a small swirl in front of Medwick before drifting away.

Medwick turns and walks towards the rescued Gingoile.

'My dear, old friend,' Medwick says as he hugs him.

'It's been far too long, Medwick,' replies the old Gingoile.

'We tried so many times,' continues Medwick, 'but without the leaves and Eddie and his friends, we just couldn't free you.'

'Yes,' says the Gingoile turning to face me, 'Eddie and his friends.'

There's cheering and applause all around. We all look at each other a little dumbfounded.

'I assume,' I say as the applause dies down, 'that this Gingoile *is* the formula? After all, we weren't really looking for a Gingoile. We were looking for a formula; either written down, or in a liquid form, or something!'

'I'm sorry,' says Medwick as he walks over and takes my hands in his, 'I felt that telling you it was a rescue mission might have been too much for you.'

'So, where is the formula?' asks Liz.

'In my head, Miss,' replies the Gingoile.

'Why?' asks Carrot.

'It was the only way I could stay alive,' says the Gingoile.

It goes quiet.

'I think we need to explain a few things,' says Medwick. 'Lead us back to the Palace, please, Herf.'

'Certainly, Medwick,' replies the ever-eager Herf.

'And double, no, treble the guard, please, Herf. We don't want any immediate revenge catching us out.'

'Yes, Medwick.'

Medwick goes to leave, before I stop him.

'One thing, Medwick,' I say, 'I don't even know the name of the Gingoile who we rescued!'

Medwick just smiles one of his moustache-covered smiles and looks at the Gingoile.

'Hello, Eddie' says the rescued Gingoile offering me his hand, 'I'm Krenk!'

Krenk? I look at the others.

Raised eyebrows all around!

*

.

We are now seated in quite a large room in the Palace. I don't think it's one we've been in before. I'm sat, flanked by my friends. There's also Medwick, Herf, Krenk and a few other Gingoiles seated around. Drinks are being served and a few more Gingoiles are entering through various doors.

'Krenk?' whispers Liz. 'Another brother of Krunk and Krank, do you think?'

'I'm guessing so,' I reply.

At which Krunk and another Gingoile enter the room. Krenk immediately stands and hugs Krunk and his friend, who I assume is Krank, and then they start speaking Gingoilian. Quite rapidly!

'I think they'll need a moment, or two,' says Medwick, 'they're brothers and it has been over a hundred years!'

Just a moment, or two, after a hundred years!!

'I thought they might be brothers,' I say, 'Krunk, Krank and Krenk?'

'That's correct, Master Eddie,' he continues, 'well worked out!'

There's a twinkle in his eye. Was he being sarcastic!? I just smile.

'When are Krink and Kronk coming?' asks Carrot.

'I beg your pardon,' replies Medwick.

'Well,' continues Carrot, 'I was wondering if they had any more brothers and if they were called Krink and Kronk!?'

We all smile.

'No, no, no, young Carrot,' comes Medwick's reply. 'Krink and Kronk aren't Gingoile names. They're just silly names!'

Medwick stands up to greet Krunk and Krank. We all laugh quietly at Carrot who replies with a shrug!

Medwick and the three Ks soon take their seats opposite us.

'Would you like us to explain everything?' asks Medwick.

'Yes, please,' I politely reply as I sense my friends all nodding.

'Well,' begins Medwick, 'I'll keep it as brief as I can. You know I told you that 114 years ago Zendorf forced everyone to take a drug stopping them from having babies?'

'Yes,' I reply.

'Well,' continues Medwick, 'it was Krenk who invented the drug.'

'What!?'

'It's true,' starts up Krenk. 'I was kidnapped and told to engineer the drug.'

'I thought the Thargs invented it,' says Liz.

'Huh,' chips in Herf grumpily, 'they couldn't invent anything!'

'Thank you, Herf,' interjects Medwick.

'Herf's correct,' says Krenk, 'they couldn't invent anything. That's why they kidnapped me.'

'They couldn't even get that right, could they!?' says Herf.

'No,' replies Krenk, 'you're quite right, Herf. They got hold of Krank first, didn't they?'

Krank nods.

'But we then agreed to swap him for me.'

'So, why make the drug?' asks Becky.

'Because, if I didn't, they would continue to defeat us in battle. It was a way of creating some sort of peace.'

'Which would end in the Gingoile race eventually disappearing,' says Carrot.

'Yes,' says Medwick stepping in swiftly, 'but Krenk did have the formula for the antidote.'

'He had to have that for the Thargs,' replies Carrot.

'True,' says Medwick.

'What I don't get,' says Carrot, 'and I never have; is why the Thargs took the drug at all. Why not just the Gingoiles?'

Good question, mate!

'Herf!' calls Medwick.

'Well,' says Herf stepping forward.

He says no more.

'Well, what?' says Carrot.

'Just well,' says Herf.

We all look at each other. Herf usually loves to talk so why is he just saying "well"?

'Please expand, Herf,' says Medwick.

'Certainly, Medwick,' says Herf. 'To guarantee all the Gingoiles got the drug, they put it in the well. Well, all the wells, actually. In fact, they put it in all water sources; rivers and so on. The downside of this was them drinking it themselves. That's why Krenk was told to create an antidote.'

Herf sits back down.

There're a few moments of silence.

'I'm still not sure why you agreed to make the drug, Krenk,' says Becky.

'Nor am I,' adds Liz.

'To stop the deaths in battle,' says Krenk, 'and to buy us time!'

'You've been imprisoned at The Dark Castle for 114 years!' I exclaim.

'Exactly,' replies Krenk. 'I bought plenty of time!'

'How did you survive?' asks Liz.

'By refusing to give them the antidote,' comes Krenk's reply. 'I started the whole thing off by giving them false drugs. Making them think it was working, until a Tharg or Gingoile would have a baby, at which point I had to start again. Of course, all along I knew what I was doing, but they had no idea! Finally, I had to give them the proper drug when they threatened to kill my brothers. But I refused to tell them, or write down, the formula for the antidote.'

'What did they make of that?' asks Carrot.

'Initially,' replies the Gingoile, 'they tried to force it out of me. When they realised that wasn't going to work, they had to keep me alive. I've been generally well looked after!'

'That didn't look particularly nice where we found you!' says Brian.

'Well, no,' says Krenk, 'I usually live lower down in that tower, or sometimes in the West Tower. That hidey hole is where they put me whenever there's danger.'

'How did Uncle Mark know where you'd be?' I ask.

'Well,' continues Krenk, 'I became aware of your uncle soon after he attempted to save me ten years ago. The rescue almost worked, but before they could find my hidey hole the rescue was halted in its tracks. Then, a few days later, I was aware of a light reflecting in my room in the East Tower. It was coming from the North Tower and, fortunately, my brother Krank had taught me

Morse code many years ago and I was able to communicate. It was your Uncle Mark.'

I can see Krank smiling. I still haven't heard him speak. Funny, for the brother who's an expert in languages!

'You've been communicating ever since?' I ask.

'Whenever we can.'

'You knew we were coming today?'

'Yes,' continues Krenk. 'After your uncle had made contact with you earlier today, he made contact with me. I knew I'd be taken to my hidey hole as soon as the alarm went off.'

'The GCD,' cries Medwick, 'the one your uncle made! Where is it? We can now talk to him!'

I've never seen Medwick so animated as Liz delves into one of her pockets and retrieves the pebble-like GCD.

Krunk's eyes light up as he sees the size of the GCD.

'Jerple haf kroi,' exclaims Krunk.

'It is very small,' replies Medwick.

I decide to get out the original GCD out for Krunk.

'Ah,' says Krunk, 'jar kampfle rin den gen. Nin frass bar frun!'

All the Gingoiles laugh.

'What did he say,' I ask.

'He said that his stone might be bigger, but it's the original and therefore the best!' replies Medwick.

We all join in with the laughter.

'Talk to your uncle, Eddie,' says Medwick. 'Talk to him.'

I return the original GCD to my pocket and take the smaller one from Liz.

'Uncle,' I say. 'Are you there? It's Eddie.'

I hold my breath as I await a reply.

'Try again,' says Carrot.

'Uncle,' I repeat. 'Hello! It's Eddie here.'

Still no response.

'Can I try,' says Liz holding out her hand.

'Sure,' I say as I return the pebble to my sis.

'Uncle Mark,' says Liz, 'it's Elizabeth here. Are you ok?

Silence.

Tears start to stream down Liz's cheeks.

'Uncle?' I take the pebble from her and slide it into my pocket as both Becky and I hug Liz.

'What does that mean?' asks Carrot.

'It possibly means that your uncle is probably under increased guard at the moment and unable to respond,' comes Medwick's reply.

'Are you sure?' asks Liz as she dries her eyes.

'Unfortunately not,' is Medwick's unhelpful reply, 'but it will be even more important that they keep your uncle alive now.'

'Why?' asks Brian.

'Because, young Brian,' continues Medwick, 'not only do we have Krenk and the formula; we also have Eddie. Remember our conversation about them having to keep Mark alive if they want control of the Ruler? Whilst Eddie and Liz are free, the Thargs have to keep Mark alive otherwise they will have lost everything.'

Medwick smiles at me.

'So; what now?' I ask.

'You go home, Master Eddie,' is Medwick's somewhat surprising reply.

'Home!?' I echo.

'Yes. Home.'

'No,' cries out Liz, 'we can't go now. We have Uncle Mark to rescue.'

Medwick approaches Liz and takes her hands in his.

'That must wait for another day,' he says.

'But, why?' she asks.

'As I said, Liz, your uncle will be safe. It is Eddie, and you, who now need protecting.'

'We've been protecting Eddie all along,' says Carrot.

'I know you have,' replies Medwick, 'but now Zendorf and the Thargs definitely know Eddie's here, he needs even more protection. After all; if they capture Eddie, and indeed Elizabeth, we'll be in trouble again.'

'And then they might start bartering to swap you with me,' adds Krenk, 'so that I can make another formula and the vicious circle will just start again.'

We all sit in silence for a while.

'Can't we stay?' asks Liz. 'Everything here does only last six seconds in our world.'

'True,' replies Medwick, 'but, as I say, now everyone knows you're all here, I can't guarantee your safety.'

Four sad and sorrowful faces are once more glued on me.

'The safest place for you all is at home,' says Medwick, 'not in The Realm. We'll make it seem to the Thargs that you're still here. Send them on a bit of a wild goose chase. That'll give us time to release the antidote into the water. Then we'll decide on how to rescue Mark. How does that sound.'

I look at my tired looking friends. They give me various smiles and nods.

'Ok,' I say, 'let's go home.'

'Assemble a guard,' calls out Medwick, 'we'll leave for my cottage immediately!'

'Why so soon?' asks Becky.

'Before the Thargs can start to send out scouting parties, is best.'

*

Here we are. Back at Medwick's cottage. We left Krenk with his brothers to start on the formula and came back via the zones very rapidly, with several Gingoile guards alongside Medwick and Herf. Flounge came out to greet us by the well; topping us up with food! The guard are outside and we're in the room with a brick missing from the wall, with Medwick and Herf.

'What shall I do with these,' I say to Medwick whilst holding out the two GCDs.

'Keep them,' answers Medwick.

'Doesn't Krunk want them?'

'He knows that the small one is only designed to work when you or Liz are holding it. Even he won't be able to get that one to work. And as for the bigger one; keep it as a souvenir!'

'Thanks,' I reply. 'Will either of them work across Realms? You know; from our world to yours?'

'The large one definitely won't,' says Medwick. 'As for the other one. No idea!'

We all smile.

'Now, let's not make this any harder than we need to,' says Medwick. 'We know we'll see you all again.'

'But, when?' asks Liz. 'How will we know when you need us?'

'Don't worry. You'll know!' comes the mysterious reply.

'Say goodbye to everyone, Herf.'

'Yes, Medwick.'

Herf silently hugs us in turn. By the time he hugs me I can see tears running down his face and nestling in his moustache.

Goodbye, Eddie,' he says quietly. 'Take care.'

'You, too, Herf,' I manage to say whilst trying to hold back the tears.

As Medwick quietly makes his way round us I see there's no point in holding back the tears. Everyone is crying, including Brian.

'Goodbye, Master Eddie,' says Medwick, 'and thank you.'

'You're welcome,' I reply feebly. 'Goodbye, Medwick.'

I walk to the wall, taking hold of Liz's hand on the way.

'Everyone take a hand!' I say.

A chain is formed and I look through the hole in the wall.....

'Goodbye.....................'

# Chapter Seventeen

And there we all are. Standing by the wall.

'Just gone eight,' says Carrot who's immediately checking his watch.

'Same day?' I ask.

'Yes,' says Carrot as he presses a button on his watch.

I sit down and lean back on the wall.

'You ok, Bro?' asks Liz who seems to still be holding back her tears.

'I think so,' I reply, 'it's just been quite a long six seconds!'

Everyone laughs.

'You can say that again!' says Carrot as he sits down next to me.

Liz, Becky and Brian all follow suit and join me on the ground; leaning against the wall.

'Should we put the brick back in the wall?' asks Brian.

We all stare at the brick.

'I don't think there's much point,' I say, 'it's only me that can go through the gap.'

'And anyone you're holding hands with!' adds Becky with a smile.

'True,' I say. 'But anyone not in contact with me will be fine!'

There's a pause as we all seem unable to comprehend the days and hours that have happened in those six seconds.

'We did just do all that, didn't we?' asks Brian.

'We certainly did!' I reply.

'And if you need to go back to help rescue your uncle, or anything at all, you will ask me to come, won't you, Eddie?'

I can't believe he really needs to ask that!

'Of course!' I say. 'You're part of the team! We certainly wouldn't have achieved anything without you!'

'Quite right!' says Liz.

Followed by an "Absolutely" from Becky and a "You're one of us!" from Carrot.

'Thanks, Eddie,' smiles Brian. 'Thanks everyone!'

Everyone is taking in the surroundings. Back on Earth! It's all the same as before, but oh so different. I look at my friends; old and new. We're the same five people that went into The Realm, but everything has changed. I feel that The Realm has brought the best out of me. I hope they all feel the same.

Eventually Brian gets up.

'I think I'm gonna head home now,' he says.

'Ok,' I reply as I stand up.

'See you at school, tomorrow?' he asks.

'Sure!' I say.

Brian offers me his hand. I shake it in as manly a way as I can. I think Brian goes gently with his grip! We share a smile before he turns and trudges off down the hill.

'Bye, Brian,' call out Liz, Becky and Carrot.

Brian turns and smiles.

'Bye, everyone,' he says before continuing his descent.

'I suppose we should all go home,' suggests Liz after a few moments.

'Guess so,' I reply as I stand up, 'although Mum might wonder why we're back so soon!'

Everyone laughs.

'I'll go home via Becky's,' says Liz.

'Ok,' I say.

We all share goodbyes as me and Carrot watch Liz and Becky disappear down the hill.

'Do you want me to walk home with you, Eddie?' offers Carrot.

'I think you've protected me enough, Carrot' I say with a smile. 'I'll be ok, thanks.'

'Ok, mate,' replies Carrot whilst patting me on the shoulder. 'See you at school, tomorrow.'

'Bye, Carrot.'

He waves as he makes his way down the hill.

I turn to look at the wall. I see the hole in it and feel like I should take another look through it. I mustn't. What if I get too close and it sucks me back through? I can hear Medwick now. "Haven't you had enough, Master Eddie?" he'd say.

I think I'll go home for now.

*

It's my birthday! Six days have passed since our 'six seconds' in The Realm. As it's a school night, Mum said I should just have a few friends around for a birthday tea. I have to say that, apart from Carrot, she was rather surprised when I asked if Liz, Becky and Brian could join us. She said, through a rather quizzical expression, that it was up to me.

We've had pizza. Carrot offered to cook it, but Mum said she was fine! Then jelly, ice cream and birthday cake. Mum said how grown up we were. Poor Mum. If only she knew. Liz and I *so* want to say something about her brother, but we are sticking to our agreement with our uncle not to tell her anything about him. It's so difficult. Almost painful.

We're now sat in the lounge. My birthday presents are on the coffee table. Darts from Carrot (what a surprise!) and a football from Brian, signed by his uncle! Liz and Becky clubbed together to buy me a book entitled 'Unexplained Phenomena'. I wonder what gave them the idea to buy that! I've also placed my wooden box, the map and the two GCDs on the table.

'Nice touch,' says Carrot pointing at the things on the table. 'Putting those with your birthday presents.'

'Well,' I reply, 'I see them as birthday presents from The Realm!'

'What's the piece of paper?' asks Brian.

'That's the map,' I reply.

'But it's blank!' exclaims Brian.

'I know,' I say. 'It's a map of The Realm. A map of any part of The Realm. But it doesn't work here. It's just blank.'

'Oh,' is Brian's brief reply.

'You better not lose it,' says Becky.

'True,' I say. 'I'll put it back in the box where it belongs.'

I slide the lid off the box and place the map inside. As I close the lid it feels strange.

'That's weird,' I say.

'What is?' asks Liz.

'The lid,' I continue. 'When I closed it, it seemed to seal itself. Look!'

Liz takes the box from me.

'There's no sign of the lid, anymore,' she says as she hands it back to me.

'That's exactly how it was before we went to The Realm, now,' says Carrot.

'I guess it means the map is safe and hopefully we can retrieve it when we're back in The Realm,' I add.

'When do you think that will be?' asks Becky.

'No idea,' I reply, 'that's why I try and keep the box and GCDs close. Just in case....'

'We don't even know if they work across Realms, do we?' says Liz.

'We don't know about the GCDs,' I say, 'but we know the box works.'

'The box was designed to work once,' says Liz. 'Will it work again?'

I just shrug.

'Medwick never did get around to answering *my* question, did he?' says Brian.

'Which question was that, Brian?' I ask.

'The one about why humans are the rulers in The Realm.'

'That's true,' says Liz, 'he said he'd "elaborate at a later date"!'

'We're gonna have to make sure we see him at a later date then, aren't we, so that he has time to elaborate!'

Everyone smiles.

Unless Uncle Mark somehow has children of his own, then Liz, or me, or both of us, *will* see Medwick again at some point. As the new ruler.

'Right,' says Carrot jumping up and heading to a shelf of DVDs. 'I spy a film we should watch.'

'Really?' I say. 'But that's Dad's collection of old films!'

'Exactly,' he says, 'we need to watch the film that saved my life!'

He turns around holding up Spartacus!

We all laugh.

'Well,' says Becky, 'we did tell Brian we'd show him it!'

'Yep!' says Brian.

'Put it on then, Carrot,' I say.

We all settle down to watch the film.

The word 'SPARTACUS' fills the TV screen.

You might be Spartacus; but I'm Eddie Ross and I have my own Realm.

Did my box just give off a faint glow...?

## About the author

Ashley Burgoyne is originally from Luton, but has been a resident of North Norfolk for over thirty years. He is a playwright, a poet and the creator and writer of 'Crocodile Keith and his Shiny, White Teeth!' When not writing, Ashley can be found composing and teaching the classical guitar.

## Other books by Ashley Burgoyne

For children:

- **Crocodile Keith and his Shiny, White Teeth!**
  An educational, rhyming picture book for young children, with illustrations by Matthew Doyle

Plays:

- **The Village Hall** – A Comedy Play
- **The Hotel Room** – A Comedy Play
- **Twisted Tales** – Two One-Act Plays, co-written with Melissa Collin

Poetry:

- **The Sublime and the Ridiculous** – A poetic meander through life, co-written with Melissa Collin

Non-fiction:

- **From Len to Lil with Love and a Lick.**
  Letters across London during The Blitz.

Printed in Great Britain
by Amazon